SPLENDID DAWN

SPLENDID DAWN

BY
YVONNE ST. CLAIRE

LONDON : THE EPWORTH PRESS

THE EPWORTH PRESS
(FRANK H. CUMBERS)
25–35 City Road, London, E.C.1

MELBOURNE   CAPE TOWN
NEW YORK   TORONTO

PRINTED IN GREAT BRITAIN BY RICHARD CLAY AND COMPANY, LTD.,
BUNGAY, SUFFOLK

CHARACTERS

Historic—

Sir William Johnson, Col. Guy, and Mrs. Johnson; Chief Joseph Brant; Mrs. Brant; Catherine of the Turtles; King George III, the Prince, and Nobility of England, mentioned; Chief Little Abraham; Rev. Dr. Stewart.

Fictional—

Sergeant Dennis Jenks (various minor characters, such as Oneida Chief, brother of Moon Bow).

HISTORIC AUTHORITY

Ryerson Press History Reader, Joseph Brant. Records of Daily Star Library, Toronto. Family history of Mills and Gage Families (lent to me). Also the 'United Empire Loyalists', a MS. in possession of the Beasley family, Toronto. All these references with permission of possessors.

CHAPTER I

Sir William Johnson's dignified Sergeant-at-Arms stared over his stiff stock at the amazing scene before him. Never in all his eighteen months of fairly continuous duty outside the door of Sir William's Council Room had he beheld anything quite like it! True, from his vantage point at the head of the great stairway of Johnson Hall he had a good view of all comers; he had witnessed state entries through the main doorway of both friend and foe, European diplomat and Indian spokesman. He had seen the triumphal entries of soldiers of the King whose work was well done; he had seen traitors and deserters brought in the same way, when hauled back captive to their just deserts. The picturesque, but none the less impressive arrival of Indians suing for peace or clemency, and others, proud in their enjoyment of British protection, coming with their periodic reports. The spectacle of a man and boy struggling with each other as they mounted the stairway was something entirely novel, however, and Sergeant Jenks, in his outraged astonishment, very nearly forgot his soldier's part.

'Arrah thin! An' is ut a siege we're having!' he ejaculated, then remained still, observing the newcomers.

The man was stronger, of course, and despite the lad's struggles continued mounting the stairway higher and higher, dragging him on, and as they emerged from the cool gloom of the lower hall into the light of the upper windows, Jenks had a good look at them.

'Indians!' he thought, 'and of the Mohawk tribe.'

Then he went on wondering what should cause such a

7

display of strong feeling between two of a breed usually so stoical and dignified. The man was in full war regalia, a particularly bronzed specimen, with strong limbs and, even for an Indian, particularly brutal-looking hands. But it was the lad who attracted the Sergeant, he was so amazingly different!

He must have been about thirteen, tall for his age, and slenderly, though beautifully, built, with a proud head poised on a long, muscular neck. Even then he bore the air of one born to command; also, his skin, though sunburnt and obviously unwashed, was much lighter than that of his companion. Only his flashing dark eyes, hawk nose, and prominent chin betokened the Indian breed. 'Else', thought the Sergeant, stepping forward to interfere, 'he might pass for a young gentleman from Old France, whom in the Northlands now they call the French-Canadians.'

'Avast there!' he barked suddenly, halting the couple as they reached the stair head. 'Phwat's goin' on here? Hast forgot, ye spalpeen, in whose house ye stand?'

The lad said nothing. He stood panting in his captor's grip, sweating profusely, his face and neck a dull red beneath the forest tan, but the man answered in a slow, painful attempt at the English tongue.

'Nikus Brant sorry. Nickus Brant would see Great White Chief, ask pardon.'

'Humph! Ye need to! But dost have to bring this forest wildcat clawing an' spitting up our Grand Stairway to do that?' demanded the Sergeant sharply.

'Forest cat! My brother sayeth well!' retorted the Indian with something like a snarl, and shaking the lad roughly. 'It is for his shame that I am come!'

'Well, don't abuse him,' cautioned the Sergeant authoritatively. 'Begorra! If it's Sir William's justice ye're seekin', he won't thank ye fer hangin' the culprit first an' then findin' out if he's guilty, ye know!'

So saying, and with a glance of no great favour, Sergeant Jenks knocked on a nearby door, and being given permission to enter, approached Sir William's desk and laid the matter before him.

Sir William Johnson, Major-General of the British Forces of New York, Colonel of the Six Nations, and Superintendent of Indian Affairs, was at that time a man of about fifty. Tall, fair-skinned, and clear-eyed, with a noble forehead and a singularly gentle mouth, he blended with his wise administration of his Redskin dependants a whimsical vein of humour, which helped him to smooth out many an intricate situation. His methods were, at times, racy to the verge of the burlesque, yet on other occasions he displayed such adroit penetration and high courage as to gain many a point he aimed at, by sheer audacity. He was a handsome man, and a lonely one, too, for Lady Johnson had died some five years before, and he presided over the baronial splendours of Johnson Hall alone. That solitude was broken now, however, by the return of his daughter, Catherine, from a finishing school in Montreal, and she was to take her place by her father's side as hostess of the mansion. Sir William was feeling particularly complacent that morning, for the return of the gentle Catherine, her presence at the breakfast-table, her influence already making itself felt in the administration of domestic affairs, pleased and comforted him.

'There is no hand in the home like a woman's,' he reflected comfortably. 'I've been a solitary man for years, but surely things will be different now.'

It was at this instant that Sergeant Jenks presented himself and told his tale—briefly and soldier-like at first, and then with low asides, which, if not according to strict military procedure, had a value all their own, as Sir William from past experience knew well.

' So-o-o,' he reflected, having thought awhile, ' thou art not too favourably impressed with him, eh, Jenks? '

' No, Sir William, not with the man,' returned the soldier bluntly.

' And with the lad? '

' I cannot say, sorr. Methinks without his captor's grip an' in his own senses he—— '

' And that captor is likely bullying him now,' interrupted Sir William. ' Admit them, Jenks, and look ye, enter yourself, and stand within the door.'

Sergeant Jenks saluted, and withdrew, to return almost instantly with the Indians, man and boy, whom he hustled forward till they stood directly in front of Sir William's desk, and then he took his own place at the door.

The boy was not resisting now, though the other still held him fast. But he was looking round the room, curiously, almost reverently; and then his gaze was caught and held by Sir William's keen blue eyes.

He appeared to recognize the man. ' How now, Nickus Brant! ' he said, surprised, and glancing from one to the other, ' What would ye here, and why the prisoner? '

' For his shame I come,' returned the Indian, speaking in accents in which servility seemed mingled with rage. ' He hath abused my hearth, caused rebellion in my wigwam. I would have slain him with my own hand, but that—— '

' Thou didst most wisely think better of it, especially

knowing mine edict concerning such,' interposed Sir William smoothly, but with blue eyes very hard.

' Yet he is mine own,' retorted the Indian somewhat sullenly, ' and speaks not the White Man's Law that an Englishman may do what he will—with his own.'

' Only to a point,' returned Sir William, speaking now in the smooth drawl of the Mohawks. ' No man, be he Red or White, holds in his own hands the power to kill or keep alive—even his own son.'

' I am not his son,' broke in the lad, suddenly, but decidedly.

Nickus Brant uttered an exclamation of wrath, and shook him so furiously that Sir William sprang to his feet.

' Have done, Nickus. Have done, I say, and take thy hand from off thy tomahawk. Right off. Now release him—stand farther away from him; farther yet. Zounds, man! Look at the marks of thy great fingers on his shoulder. Wouldst tear the living flesh from off his bones?'

Reluctantly he who was called Nickus Brant stepped aside, and Sir William stared, with very real interest now, at the supposed culprit. There was silence for a while as the grave blue eyes of the baronet met the dark ones of the lad; then he spoke again, still using the Indian tongue.

' What is thy name, lad, and what hast thou done?'

The proud head slowly lifted, as though attracted by the note of kindliness that voice contained. The compressed lips parted, then, ere he could speak, Nickus Brant cut in:

' His name is Joseph Brant, sir; Joseph Brant, and he hath rebelled against the lawful authority of me—his father.'

' I bade thee be silent, Nickus,' retorted Sir William sharply, and he noticed the sudden darkening of the lad's face. ' It doth appear to me that thou art unable to control thyself, let alone thy son—— '

' I am not his son '; again the lad's fierce assertion tore itself between clenched teeth.

' Thou art not?—Nickus, another word from thee and thou awaitest the result of this inquiry in my darkest cellar! —Thou art not his son, sayest thou, boy? Then whose son art thou?'

The lad looked up, his dark eyes staring long and searchingly into the blue ones of his questioner, as if striving to read whether interest or derision lay behind them. What he saw assured him, and he answered steadily:

' My name is Thayendanegea.'

Sir William raised his eyebrows, then nodded encouragingly:

' Meaning "Two-sticks-of-wood-bound-firmly-together." Well?'

The lad seemed to gather courage. He stepped farther away from the glowering Brant, and went on:

' And my father was Tehowaghwengaraghkin, one of the five Sachems who sailed away into the sunrise and bowed before the throne of the Great White Queen who rules there.'

' Her late Gracious Majesty Queen Anne, eh?' returned Sir William, interpreting for himself, and really surprised now. Then, as he glanced from one to the other, he felt he could not doubt the statement, for the free, proud carriage of the youth, contrasted with the lowering resentment of the man, told its own tale.

' How comest thou to be with him, then?' he asked, and again Nickus struck in:

' He liveth in my lodge, I say. I have hunted for him, killed for him, and—— '

'Is this lad thine own son, Nickus Brant?' demanded
Sir William Johnson suddenly, turning upon him, and before that stern and steady gaze the other's truculence
seemingly oozed away.

'No.' He answered at last and very reluctantly.

'And he lieth not when he claims to be the son of one of
those Five Great Ones, as he says?'

'It—it may be so—I cannot tell.'

Sir William stood silent for a moment, staring at him,
growing disapproval in his gaze, and Sergeant Jenks was
frankly curious. The lad's breast was heaving, and he was
struggling manfully not to cry. Then Sir William went
on:

'And the boy's mother—thy squaw today, is she not?—
I thought so '—as the other glumly assented, ' had been wed,
but was husbandless when thou didst take her to thy Lodge?'

'It was so.'

'Then why art thou wroth with the lad for but asserting
the truth? And what sort of a father dost thou make, O
Nickus Brant, that to thee he should prefer a memory, albeit
a vague one?'

A steel-like quality had crept into Sir William's voice.
He still spoke the Mohawk tongue, but the listeners knew
the timbre well, and Sergeant Jenks' lips were pursed for an
instant, while the Indian openly cringed.

'It is not that, O mighty Commander. It is that he doth
forget the subservience due to such lofty ones as thy people
are. What matter if his sire was of the Five Sachems or no?
I would have him humble in the servitude of our White
Masters. To fetch and carry for them, and—— '

'Have done with thy lick-spittling, Nickus Brant!'
interrupted Sir William, sharply. 'I like it not, for it

rings not true. Many there be who talk glibly with their tongues while in their hearts there speaks other—— '

Just then came an interruption. The boy, finding himself forgotten, leaped towards the door with the speed of a young stag. Even Sergeant Jenks was unprepared, and the lad twisted past him, knocking his cherished musket from his grasp, and before he could draw breath was through the door and dashing down the stairs.

Nickus Brant was only a second behind him. With a roar in which hate and triumph were horribly blended, he leaped after him, snatching his tomahawk from his belt, and striking at his quarry with every step. Had any blow reached its mark the lad's history would have ended abruptly, but the tomahawk only bit deep and ever deeper into the polished balustrade of the great stairway as they dashed on. Sergeant Jenks was hotly in pursuit of Brant, of course, and Sir William himself ran out and stood at the top of the stairs. It was a furious race while it lasted, but at the bottom it ended as suddenly as it began, for a likely-looking young fellow of about twenty years old leaped between the pursuer and his prey, and by a well-directed upper cut stretched the man on his back at the foot of the stairs.

Sergeant Jenks was on him in a twinkling and had wrenched the tomahawk from his grasp. The newcomer, holding the lad in a strong but not unkind grip, and speaking soothingly, tried to reassure him, and all this happened as Sir William came slowly down the stairs.

' Good work, Nephew Guy,' he said approvingly. ' Take care of that youngster for me. And as for thee, Nickus Brant '—here he reverted to the Mohawk tongue—' What thy grievance was I know not—and care not now, for one thing is plain to me. Thou art no more fit to father this lad than thou art to tell his tale. What! Wouldst have murdered him in my very hall! Look at yon balustrade, good oak timber I brought from our native England. For ever now it must bear those marks, tokens of thy insensate rage. One thing is clear to me. In thine heart thou art minded either to kill or shame the child, who is, I do suspect, the son of thy one-time rival. Enough! No more words; thine apologies are as untimely as they are sickening. Thou canst go thy way, nor darken the doors of Johnson Hall again. As for the lad, see thou troublest him not again, for he is no longer in thy care. Now take thyself off!'

So saying, and beckoning the lad, now standing passive, almost dazed by the turn of events, Sir William Johnson led the way back into the Council Room.

Back at his desk, Sir William beckoned the lad to come close.

'What hadst thou done?' he questioned, placing a kindly hand on the thin shoulder. 'Speak freely, there is nought to fear.'

'He—he hates me,' muttered the lad, almost beneath his breath.

'So I noted,' returned Sir William gravely. 'Why? Because thou art not his son, or . . .?'

'I do think that is one cause, sir,' returned the lad, speaking with sudden manly directness, though of course in his own tongue, 'though that is not the only reason.'

'And what are the others?'

The boy glanced round the luxurious room with its rich furnishings and shelves of books, then he turned again to Sir William and spoke as directly as before.

'It is because of my dream,' he said.

' Thy dream? Art thou a dreamer then? '

' I am, sir, and so I would be till I can make that dream a blessed truth.'

The great soldier stared at him with more than casual interest now, but the young eyes had travelled beyond him again towards those shelves of books and the rich paintings on the walls.

' What is thy dream, Thayendanegea?' asked Sir William after a pause, and the lad answered:

' To be able to read those '—pointing to the books, ' and to know what all those '—pointing to the paintings, ' are about.'

Then while the surprised baronet stared at him he continued eagerly. ' When my father, the great Sachem, went beyond the Sunrising he saw many such things, he met many people who knew all about them and could teach others. There were those who dreamed of lifting thus the lowest of their tribes, and so I would lift my own people, by first lifting myself. I would have them stand shoulder to shoulder, gaze eye to eye with their White Brothers; I would have them know, as I would know myself, what makes the clouds to fly, the wind to blow, and the great river to run. I would have them worship the Great Spirit in wisdom, not as sheep. I would see the great places where men live in Lodges of Stone, as thou dost, and I would bow before the shining Chair where the mightiest Chief of all is sitting, even as my father once bowed. I would sail to and fro over great waters, and learn by many means how to teach my people to be better than they are. O Great White Protector, as thou hast come between me and misery, so I will swear to thee my life and servitude, if only thou wilt guide me to obtain all this.'

'Why, bless the boy! He's asking for a first-class education,' ejaculated Sir William, astonished, yet half laughing.

But the boy's face was grave. 'What is education?' he asked and the baronet faltered suddenly, for the earnest glance moved him strangely.

'Why, reading, writing, ciphering, and all the rest of it.'

'Oh, sir, wilt thou not teach me how to do all that?'

'I teach thee!' Sir William pushed his chair aside and rising, paced up and down, rubbing his head in perplexity.

'I teach thee? Zounds, lad, no schoolmaster am I. Thou wouldst need to go to school for years, learn thine A B C, thy numbers and——'

'Oh, sir, could I not do that—in between working for thee, I mean? I care not what I do. I will sleep little, eat less, if only thou wilt show me how I may learn to read—those.'

Sir William Johnson was a man of great culture and scholarship; he loved learning for learning's sake, and for a moment, following with his eyes the expressive gesture of the young Indian, barriers of race or social caste seemed forgotten. For a moment they stared at each other, the proud English gentleman, and the half-naked savage lad. Then Sir William turned again and continued pacing to and fro, and the lad's pleading gaze travelled with him. Presently he paused again.

'And thou dost wish all this for thine own sake, eh? Because of what thy father was. I suppose thou wouldst be Heap Big Chief—as he was, eh?'

The lad smiled faintly, then shook his head. 'I would be,' he answered, 'such as when I am grown, I may call thee "Brother", and may so instruct my people that they may all thy people brethren also.'

'H'm. Doubtful honour,' retorted Sir William, but in

B

English; then suddenly he reached towards his desk and picked up a small bound book.

'Take this, Thayendanegea,' he said, pressing the volume into the lad's ready hands. 'Today is the first day of summer. If by the end of the season thou canst come to me and read aloud, in English, but one chapter of that book, I will grant thee thine heart's desire.'

'Oh, sir—thou meanest . . .'

'I mean that I will send thee to school, to a place of learning where thou mayest know about all these things. And when thou hast remained there long enough thou shalt return to me, and read all the books this room contains.'

'Oh, sir!' The racial stoicism was forgotten. He clasped his protector's hands, pressed them to his forehead, his thin breast, his quivering lips; and he picked the book up almost reverently, and turned to depart. Then as suddenly his face clouded.

'Alas, it is in thy strange tongue. I do not understand a single word. How may I read with none to teach me?'

'That is thy business,' returned Sir William, seating himself once more at his desk and with a gesture of dismissal.

Thayendanegea moved towards the door, book in hand, puzzled gaze upon it. Then at the threshold he turned and looked once more beseechingly at his patron.

'Well?' inquired that gentleman, whose sympathy was more deeply stirred than he cared to own.

'At least, O my protector,' pleaded the lad, 'tell me what you call this mystic book which some day I WILL learn.'

'That may or may not be,' returned Sir William with affected carelessness, 'and as such the title can mean little to thee. But I will tell, if it aids thee aught. That book is a copy of the Gospel according to St. Mark.'

CHAPTER II

THE stately home of Sir William Johnson, since described as 'the only baronial mansion now standing in the United States', was a large edifice standing foursquare within spacious grounds, and flanked on either side by two formidable forts. Men said these solid stone blockhouses were connected with the main building by secret passages deep beneath the earth. Certainly, though the family well—stone-coped and occupying a conspicuous place in the park-like plateau before the Hall—might easily be contaminated by any besieging force, it was declared of little importance save for watering cattle, and for the convenience of visiting companies, in times of peace, and that, for the simple reason —or so it was whispered—that beneath the lowest cellars of the Hall itself was another well containing an unfailing supply. Nobody knew for certain about the matter, for Sir William lived in baronial style, ruling his servants and dependants with an inflexible, if kindly, hand, and any display of undue curiosity or gossip would be sternly checked.

Few dared to risk his wrath, though many thrived by reason of his kindness. He was a fearless fighting man, implacable to his enemies, generous to his friends, an impartial judge, and a conscientious administrator of the law. For this reason he was popular amongst his brothers-in-arms, and he was revered adviser and trusted guide to the Red Men, awakening as they were from long centuries of primeval elementalism from which the alliance of the Many Hearths Confederacy, as the Six Nations Agreement was sometimes called, was but a crude, if progressive step. He rejoiced in many titles, Colonel of the Six Nations, Superintendent of Indian Affairs, and more than anything else the Red Men's Friend, for he understood them, as he himself was understood, and had many a time smoothed, by his adroit tact, the slippery track both Easterner and Westerner must take before they could agree in common brotherhood.

Johnson Hall stood in spacious grounds, well kept and with more than mere utility in their tasteful design. The lawns, which were also the camping grounds, were velvety grassed plateaux overlooked by the front windows of the Hall itself, and within easy range of the forts. This natural Council Chamber, encircled as it was by stately locust trees, provided ample space for the periodic assemblage of the Indian leaders, and their followers. The ground to the left of the Hall sloped down towards the creek and Sir William's Grist Mill, near which were the quarters of his slaves and servants, and between this and the shadow of the Hall itself, lay My Lady's Rose Garden, a sheltered place of grassy walks and mossy seats, which ever since his wife's death, Sir William had carefully preserved in all its loveliness against the time of his daughter's return from school.

That happy day had come now, and My Lady's Rose Garden was again the topic of conversation among the servants, especially those whose duty it was to tend it. It was a dewy afternoon in early summer, the spring rains so lately abated had not yet lost their influence on the budding, breathing earth, the creek in the distance, full to capacity, almost indeed in flood, was purling along at a great rate, making the responsive mill wheel spin with a

merry splash. Already, venturesome rosebuds were beginning to burst their green encasements and take shy glances
at the warming world around them, while among the
well-kept borders late spring flowers glimmered in abun-
dance, already attracting the ever-industrious bees, and
stimulating the robin and bob-o-link to much musical
effort.

Perhaps it was the combination of sound and colour that
drew him thither, or perhaps a desire to get away from
the bustle of things, that caused Thayendanegea, his first
day's work accomplished, to steal cautiously there, bent on a
few moments puzzlement with his book. It never left his
possession, and he had vowed within himself that it never
should, though how to read it was another matter. In a
deferential way he had sought among his fellow servants
for someone who would teach him, and at first he met with
laughter, off-hand, though not unkindly meant, and after a
while, to his surprise, a chance word from Sergeant Jenks
disclosed the fact that very few of the servants, or soldiers
stationed there, could either read or write. All indeed,
though in a similar plight to himself, seemed little concerned
about it, but as Sir William never encouraged callousness
or a bullying disposition among his employees, though the
Indian lad received scant help, he received much brusque, if
well-meant advice. ' Strengthen thine arm, lad, and forget
useless book-learning ! ' advised one. ' Fear God and keep
your powder dry,' advised another, unconsciously uttering
words which would embody a famous quotation later on,
and Sergeant Jenks who hailed from Northern Ireland,
patted him encouragingly on the head and remarked, ' An'
phwat for would ye be spendin' yer blessed eyes on a poor little
printed page whin they might be takin' a squint along a

musket-barrel, begorra? Schoolin' will only give ye a headache, I'm thinkin', and phwat could it be givin' ye more?'

Thayendanegea did not attempt to answer. He crept away through the gardens as soon as he could, worming his way among the rose bushes, till he halted near a sort of natural platform flanked by flowering shrubs, yet overlooking the valley, the mill stream, and a panorama of country beyond. It contained a tiny shelter and a rustic seat, but he was too absorbed to note detail, the place appealed to him because it was quiet and the moss-encrusted rock would make a good table whereon, with a carefully sharpened stick, he might copy some of the strange characters in the book and so try to understand them.

It was a heavy task. To his untutored eyes the a's and the s's, the r's and the t's looked discouragingly alike, and at last Thayendanegea flung the useless stick from him, and bending his face upon his hands, gave a hard, dry sob.

There was a rustle beside him, a sudden, quick footfall, and then a light, soft hand was resting on his head.

'My poor boy,' said a grave, sweet voice, 'What is it that grieveth thee so?'

Thayendanegea looked up, and he thought he had never seen a face more beautiful than that which bent over him now. Fair of brow, clear of eyes, with sweet, regular features, a firm though humorous mouth, and an air of dignified repose, strangely yet most attractively pervaded the personality of one so young.

Catherine Johnson at that time was about eighteen. From her father's Irish ancestry she had inherited her tall, yet slight form, and faultless complexion, while from her

English mother she had gained the clear, calm, blue eyes, and the wealth of golden hair that seemed to frame her stately head like a nimbus. She looked the personification of womanly sweetness as she stood there, that early summer's afternoon, in a light green silk gown, a sun hat over her bright curls, and by her side, Roland, the large white staghound, which followed her everywhere.

'My poor boy,' she said again in such kind accents that he thought she was singing, 'What aileth thee? Why art thou weeping so, and what is thy despair?'

Thayendanegea could understand the English tongue better than he could speak it, yet even so her cultured accents confused him, though her kind looks urged him on. At last he brushed a grimy wrist across his eyes, and rising on one knee held out the book.

'Book hold talk,' he said. 'Thayendanegea wants talk book.'

'Dost mean thou wouldst have someone read that to thee?' queried Catherine, puzzled likewise and taking it from his hand.

'Yes—no, Thayendanegea read,' said the boy laboriously. But Catherine was still at a loss. 'Thou wouldst read it—to me?' she hazarded.

Again the dark head shook. 'Yes—no. Thayendanegea read no—and Thayendanegea weep.'

Further guessing on Catherine's part was unnecessary, however, for another quick step sounded near them, and young Guy Johnson came in sight.

'Hulloa! What have we here?' he demanded, though not unkindly, and as the lad scrambled to his feet in some confusion, Catherine, detaining him gently with a touch on his arm, explained the predicament.

Guy Johnson could speak the Mohawk language as fluently as his own, and so with a few minutes of questions and answers the story was told. Then he turned to Catherine. 'It doth appear, sweet Cousin Cathie,' he said, 'That thy father's unique humour is in evidence here. He challenges the lad to read any one chapter of this book before the summer ends, and then, should he succeed, hath promised him his heart's desire, which is, apparently, a chance of education at the Indian School.'

'He might as well have set him to scale the clouds,' ejaculated Catherine, half indignantly. 'Dost know thy letters, boy?'

Thayendanegea would not have understood, but Guy Johnson obligingly translated, and so he replied, using his own soft speech, and glancing now and again gratefully at his interpreter.

'Alas, sweet lady, I am but a poor ignorant boy, I know little, but I am willing, ah! so willing to learn. Wilt thou not tell me how I may do it? It is not for myself alone I plead, but for my people. If I can be taught myself, then some day I will be a great warrior like—like him,' pointing in the direction of the Hall, 'and then I will raise my people to be great.'

Faithfully Guy translated, for Catherine's benefit, and though he might have regarded the whole matter as a joke, he was checked by a sudden grave glance from her bright eyes. So all at once he grew grave also, then remarked in a swift aside, 'Thou hast undertaken a hard task, boy.'

'I know it,' sighed the Indian, 'but I will do anything. I will work, fight, endure, I care not how much, if only there may be found one to teach me.'

'What art saying?' demanded Catherine, prettily in-sistent, and Guy told her.

She looked thoughtfully at them both for a little while, then with an imperious gesture, requested the young officer to translate what she would say.

'Thayendanegea, wilt thou devote thy love and loyalty to one whom I shall name, if I see to it that thou dost obtain thy heart's desire?' she asked.

'Yes, lady, yes—to thyself most willingly.'

Catherine smiled, shaking her head gently. 'It is not for myself I ask it. It is——' here she paused, her colour deepened and she glanced briefly in the direction of her cousin. The Indian boy was quick to understand.

'Thou meanest for—him?' he said, pointing to Guy, and while the gratified officer prepared to translate, himself now well aware of the blush on Catherine's cheeks. 'Oh, yes, yes, dear lady. As he is dear to thee, so shall he be to me; as he is to thee more than thy life, so will I cover him with mine!'

Seemingly Catherine did not need to have this speech translated. The boy's expressive gestures, the surprised delight on her cousin's face proved enough. And she did not deny these sudden conclusions, though she checked the outburst with quickly lifted hand. Then sitting down on the rustic bench she opened the book and beckoned the boy to her side.

'Come hither, Thayendanegea, and good Cousin Guy, be my aid in this. Thou hast found thine instructors, poor boy, for with his help, I mean to teach thee to read myself!'

The lad was soon crouching at her feet, face alight, eyes and ears attentive, and nothing loath, Guy Johnson sat down beside her.

'The Gospel according to St. Mark, eh?' he read over her shoulder. 'H'm, mine uncle might have chosen worse.'

'Indeed and indeed he chose most excellently,' she replied. 'Yes, what is it, boy?'

'What is "Gospel", and who is "St. Mark"?' asked the Indian, and when Guy translated, Catherine answered, 'The Good News, Thayendanegea, the blessed story of our most gracious Lord and Saviour Jesus Christ!'

The boy's perplexity apparently returned. 'Then is this a true story of some Great White Chief?'

'Yes,' answered Catherine, 'the greatest Chief, White, Black, or Red, who ever lived. It is He who rules the world, the winds, the waves, the flying birds, the bounding deer, and more especially the turbulent heart of Man.'

Thayendanegea's hands were clasped, his eyes gleamed excitedly. 'Greater than our spirits? Greater than the Great Manitou who lives——' He finished with a wide-flung expressive gesture, and the lady understood and answered readily, 'Yes. Greater than all the world, the sea, the sky. Truly thou hast a good text-book, poor boy. Come let us begin.'

At her gentle request, Guy Johnson produced writing materials, and pointing to the first letter of the second verse of the first chapter, Catherine uttered it slowly, copying it meanwhile, on the paper before her.

'See you here, Thayendanegea? This is A. Now, say it after me, A!'

'A-a-a!' he repeated hesitatingly, and in a slow, sweet drawl.

'Very good. Now again, A!'

'A-a-a!'

'Good. Now we will write it, and you shall repeat it over again.'

The helpful Guy placed other tablets and a pen in the lad's hand, and guiding this with his own steady one, traced the letter in capitals and small characters before him.

'Again,' urged that thorough school-mistress, 'repeat it after me, and write it over and over again.'

Again and again it was written and repeated, till the faltering hand became steady, and Thayendanegea could write and pronounce the first letter of the alphabet with reasonable ease.

'Now, the next letter,' continued Catherine, pointing to the second phrase of the same verse, 'B!'

'B-B-Be-e-e!'

'Again, B!'

'Be-e!'

She smiled encouragingly, and pointed to his tablets, 'Good. Again, and we will write it. B!'

'B,' repeated the boy, and Guy's ready hand guided his first shaky outline. Then again as his own grew bolder and more at ease, 'B.'

So through the long summer afternoon these three worked together. The young lovers, united now by a common interest, and the grateful lad who loved them now so much and listened so attentively to all they told him.

By the end of the lesson Thayendanegea had mastered at least half of the alphabet, and had learned by heart in English the first verse of the Book, 'The Beginning of the Gospel of Jesus Christ, the Son of God'!

Catherine, though but a few years older, was too wise to overload the young lad's darkened mind with too many problems. In answer to his eager questions concerning the contents of the Book, she repeated that all was true therein, and that the Lord Christ was Master of all the world, but though He was so great He wanted the love of Man, and not his servile fear. Then she promised that as Thayendanegea's understanding of the arts of reading and writing grew, so she would teach him more, revealing the Story of the Creator of the World as manifested in the Person, the Life, and the teaching of our Lord Jesus Christ.

Days sped by, and became weeks in the halcyon summer weather, and soon the alphabet was memorized, certain phonetics fitted together and Thayendanegea began to read and write laboriously, but with pride.

' And—there came—a Voice—from—Heaven, saying, "Thou-art-My-be-lov-ed Son"!' The lad looked up, ' What that the Great, Great Manitou talking to—Him?' he asked, and Catherine answered, ' Yes.'

The lad put down the Book. ' Please, lady, tell Thayendanegea something of Him now. I have laboured hard, my lady knows, and now in here '—with a natural and very significant gesture towards his own bare brown breast— ' there is something that burns to know, to—un-der-stand, what I now try to read.'

Part in Mohawk and part in English came the plea, and when Guy would have demurred, she stayed him with a gentle touch.

' Dost remember, Guy, that other darkened mind to whom the Apostle Philip was sent? That was one who "understood not" unless it should be revealed. What right have we or anyone to refuse to lift such darkness, when through our poor labours the dawn may be so splendid?'

' As thou wilt, beloved. Maybe through thy so dear enthralment, I may come to see a spark of heavenly glory also.'

So the reading and writing lessons became Scripture lessons also, and to the delight of both young people the Indian's mind, as it unfolded, disclosed such power of understanding and penetration, and such nimble reasoning, that soon their self-imposed task became a joy and an adventure.

They were acknowledged lovers now. Genial Sir William had consented to a formal engagement, also he smiled on his nephew's patronage of the Indian lad. With harmless deceit, however, they concealed from him their undertaking, or the fact that Thayendanegea now spoke some English, and could read and write quite well. This was because they both agreed that when Thayendanegea should claim fulfilment of his patron's pledge, it would be more impressive if he was fluent in all three. And so the happy summer reached its prime, and the August afternoons grew long and golden, and the group might often be found sitting together in Mary Catherine's rose arbour, on that crag of rock which overlooked the creek.

' Our good friend the Missionary arrives this evening,' remarked Guy to Catherine, as the lessons for the day ended and she handed the Book back to their pupil.

' Is it Dr. Stewart, the Master of the Indian School?' queried Catherine, with a glance at the lad, and Guy nodded.

' Yes. Maybe thy good father is not unmindful of his promise. Though I do not think that is the only reason for the good Doctor's visit here.'

' Be that as it may,' returned Catherine, rising, ' I must not forget my duties as hostess. Farewell, beloved, for just a little while, and Thayendanegea, look not apprehensive; when the time is ripe thou shalt call upon my father to redeem his pledge, and never fear but he will do so.'

The two who loved her, so differently, yet so well, stood in silence watching as the graceful figure disappeared in the direction of the Hall. Then the Indian glanced into his companion's face.

' Thou lovest her so much,' he whispered, and as Guy with a half-shamed nod turned away, he went on.

' And so, oh, so do I. Nay, hear me, friend and teacher. Because she is good I can believe in God, and though in the great world of which thou hast told me now so much, there may be evil White women as there are evil Red, still I will know that good is stronger than evil, and some day, as the flowers turn up towards the sun, so shall they all come back to Him, at last.'

What Guy might have answered to this strange declaration of faith was checked, by a lusty shout, then a confusion of tongues and running feet.

' Master Guy ! Master Guy ! Begorra, Master Guy, an' phwat may ye be a doin' of there ? '

It was Sergeant Jenks, sweating, bareheaded, and terribly out of breath. ' Away there, Master Guy, and ye, too, Injun. Thim dirty spalpeens av Apaches av well nigh smashed Dr. Stewart's party to smithereens. The good gentleman's just galloped in wid barely his life an' a change av clothes ! Into cover wid ye, man an' boy. The Indians are hot upon us, an' they're raidin' Johnson Hall ! '

CHAPTER III

JOHNSON HALL was a big, square building, perched on sturdy foundations. Altogether it possessed four storeys, including the deep-dug cellars and roomy attics high up in the roof. Also two deeply burrowed underground passages led from the Hall itself to the solid stone forts that flanked it on either side. Into these forts the livestock, horses, and hunting dogs were being rushed. The heavy, steel-encased doors were shut upon them and barricaded from within, while the men-at-arms, ascending to the upper storeys, prepared to pour shot and shell on the intruders. In the Hall itself, windows and doors were blocked in the same efficient manner, the women of the household retired to the upper storey, while from attic to ground floor alike, men-at-arms were stationed at the shuttered windows ready to give their unwelcome visitors the same vigorous reception. Guy Johnson and his companion hurried back at once to find, despite the turmoil, a cool-headed authority in control. Thayendanegea was surprised to see the Lady Catherine, calm and unafraid as the rest, directing her maids in all things to help the defenders, and herself ministering to a sorely bedraggled gentleman who, it seemed, had reached the Hall with barely his life.

'There, there, good Doctor Stewart,' said the lady as her capable hands adjusted a bandage round the badly bleeding head. 'Now drink this soothing posset, and hie thee to rest in my father's room, until thine own shall be prepared. Guy, my cousin, shall attend thee, and never heed the turmoil; we will soon send these mischief-makers packing.'

' I do thank thee for thy gentleness, fair lady,' returned
the gentleman, accepting the cordial very gratefully. Then
as he returned the empty glass, ' Yet never think that I will
lie hid like a frightened rabbit while thy people fight for
me. Grant me but time to get my breath, then find me a
good gun and direct me to thy father's side.'

' 'Tis dreadful that such things must be,' sighed Catherine,
then with kindly words she glided away, soon to be busied
in another place.

Thayendanegea watched all this with shining, eager eyes.
This was something he could understand. Rebellious Red-
men, fired by fanaticism or fire-water, seeking to massacre
or enslave the new White citizens who were obviously
usurping their land The young lad's heart swelled with
indignation. From infancy he had heard tales of their
White Brothers who, intruders though they seemed at
first, had proved to be, for the most part, the Red-man's
benefactor. His recent experience and treatment at Johnson
Hall brushed everything from his boyish mind save love
and loyalty to his new-found friends. He knew enough
to contrast their mode of living with the dirty, disease-
threatened habits of many of his race. He contrasted the
refined wisdom that dominated this household with the
superstitious cruelty that haunted his people, and with
glowing face and eyes ablaze he caught up a light musket,
and armed with his own bow and arrows, took his stand
at one of the upper windows beside burly Sergeant Jenks.

' Arrah thin, young fellow-my-lad ! ' hailed the genial
sergeant. ' Shure an' faith an' ut's glad I am to see ye true
man, an' not turned woman wid yer larnin' ! '

' Hush ! ' the boy admonished quickly, his face darkening.
But the kindly Irishman was quick to understand.

'Oh-ho! A little secret, eh? Well, hould yer whistle! I'll no be tellin'! Though how did ye think I'd not be seein' ye, when wid these two eyes I've noticed Captain Guy an' my young lady a-readin'——'

'You-will-not-tell?' interrupted Thayendanegea, speaking in hesitant English.

The sergeant stared, 'Begorra, thy larnin' travels fast, lad. No, no, I'll not be tellin' on ye!'

'A-noth-er thing,' continued the boy, using the same tongue, 'Speak-not-of-woman-that-way. Remember the Lady Catherine——'

Sergeant Jenks stared still more, then spoke in entirely different tones.

'Why, begorra! Because the Lady Catherine—whom the saints presarve,—is phwat she is, dost think that all women——?'

'Yes!' interrupted Thayendanegea, very decidedly.

'Well, Howly Mike!' ejaculated the sergeant, but there was no time for more, for the raiders burst through the surrounding forest lands, leaped over the garden boundaries, and came racing on, shouting, screaming, shooting, and brandishing their weapons as they came.

Thayendanegea's heart grew hot within him as he saw the rabble ruthlessly beating their way from the direction of the rose garden, leaving a trail of disorder, broken bushes, and trampled blossoms as they came, and with steady eye and practised hand he loosed a flight of arrows at them, so rapidly and accurately as to fell the first half-dozen and most effectively check the rest. But they rallied and came on again, and then pandemonium broke, during which the roll of muskets, the yells of the Indians, and the general tumult made the welkin ring. It did not last long, however,

c

for reinforcements arrived from the nearby settlement, and so with yells of baffled hate the raiders withdrew. But they were vicious still. They knew that the speedy relief was due to friendly Mohawk scouts who had carried the news to the British camp at the settlement, and so, as they retreated, they made short work of any stragglers of that tribe they might encounter. Not content with that, they detoured to where isolated Mohawk villages were, and soon an inter-tribal battle was raging fast and furious, and breathless scouts brought the news to Sir William and his household as they were endeavouring, after the raid, to straighten things out, and reduce the tumbled ground into something like order.

A shout from the warlike baronet brought his men-at-arms around him. A few hasty words of explanation and direction, and Sir William was on horseback, with Guy at his side, and at the head of a band of soldiers, bent on enforcing law and order and the rescue of their Indian friends. And just before the troops left the gates, hurrying up from the embattled stables, mounted on a shaggy piebald pony, bow in hand, and resolution on his face, rode the Indian princeling, Thayendanegea.

'Come along then, lad,' shouted the genial Sir William in lusty approval. 'It is after mine own heart that underneath thy golden hide there lives the soul of a cavalier.'

Off went the party, riding hard and resolutely, striving to catch up with the marauders. But they were as quick as they were cunning, and were retreating rapidly, though leaving a trail of pain and ruin behind them. It was after they had journeyed some dozen miles that they encountered the saddest sight. A prosperous Indian village, where the white man's ideal of order had been practised with skill and

success for many years, and where fruitful fields and orchards
were beginning to show results, was now reduced to ashes,
its people killed or wounded, and on the trampled ground
broken implements of peace and progress bearing mute wit-
ness to the ravages of war.   They had passed through to the
outskirts and had paused momentarily, when a groan from a
nearby culvert caught the Indian lad's quick ear.   Instantly
he was off his horse and peering through the grass, then
with a shout plunged forward and raised a bleeding and all
but motionless figure in his arms.   It was Old Chief Turtle
of the Mohawks, a man renowned even to Thayendanegea
for his wise, beneficent governing, both among his own
people and among the British, too.   Now he lay wounded
to the death, and as his life ebbed away he gasped out snatches
of information to the pitying group who bent over him.

'Through—there,' he whispered, failing hands pointing
in the direction of the forest, 'follow—they—spread—
death.   Strike—me—kill—they take squaw—papoose—go
save—— '

His head dropped, and the spirit passed from the broken
body which Thayendanegea's strong young arms held.

Laying it gently down, the lad sprang again on his horse.
'He pointed this way,' he cried, reverting to the Mohawk
tongue.   Then to Guy Johnson: 'I go—wilt follow?'
Even then he seemed no longer the half-scared stripling,
but the warrior born to command, and scarcely had the
words left his tongue than he was away, and shouting to the
men to follow. Guy Johnson rode hard after, even then
wondering at the agility with which the Indian lad guided
his pony through the treacherous bushland into the cavernous
darkness of the forest.   He seemed heedless alike of concealed root or ambushed foe, his one object, seemingly, to

come up with the slayers of the Mohawk Chief Turtle, who had ravaged a peaceful village and spread death and misery everywhere they had passed.

It was well that Captain Guy followed with such speed, for not half a mile away the lad came up with them, and then commenced a struggle so fierce and brave as it was hopelessly unequal. Half a dozen of the rebels, hideous in their war paint and mad for blood, were swarming around a little group, An Indian woman with her babe pushed behind her, struggled desperately, and Thayendanegea, with arms, legs, and body, seemed to be hitting out on all sides at once. It was a hand-to-hand struggle and the lad was bleeding from a dozen cuts, but he seemed heedless of his own hurts and fought on, knife in hand, cutting, kicking, and biting like a being possessed. Just as Guy and his men broke upon them, the woman fell, flinging herself, with her one last effort, over her child; and it would have gone hard with Thayendanegea but that Sergeant Jenks, roaring like a lusty bull, and with a strange mixture of British cheers and Irish expletives joined the fray.

'Good lad! Have at 'em! Begorra, ye dirrty spalpeens, stan' ye but still, an' I'll nail the hide o' ye to the fence! Arrah, and would ye thin! Good lad, Injun! Kick him in the gizzard! Arrah! an' would ye thin. It's yer backbone I'll be hitchin' over yer left ear, ye copperhided villain! Rule Britannia, now and forever! By the great Brian Boro, it's yer liver I'll be havin' fer me chicken feed!'

While Sergeant Jenks shouted and smote thus lustily, Guy and his men joined the fray. But the Indians scarcely waited for them. Startled by the tumultuous appearance of the Irishman, more terrified by his continued rumble of words, they no sooner saw the rest than they fled, leaving two of their number dead and a third in sorry plight, and Thayendanegea, breathless but unharmed, staggered towards the woman and tried to raise her.

'My little sister, look up,' he murmured in their own tongue. 'Look up now, for all is—— Oh, alas, my captain, look here!' This last ejaculation was in English and to the sympathetic Guy, for the woman was dead.

A half-smothered whimper roused the lad. Hastily lifting the dead mother to one side, he stooped again, and gently lifted a small bundle that squirmed and then wailed piteously.

It was a little girl of about two or three years old. Shining black hair, straight, as that of her nation's usually is, but wondrous thick and glossy, covered a round head, and a face of palest gold was lit by two sparkling brown eyes. A button nose and a puckered mouth completed the picture, while the little one, lunging with well-developed limbs, made known her distress by a lusty cry.

'All that is left!' sighed the lad, hushing her with unusual gentleness. 'All else is death. Oh! my captain, what must we do?'

'What dost thou wish, Thayendanegea?' inquired Captain Guy kindly. 'Remember, this little one owes her life to thee?'

The lad looked around at the traces of the struggle, at the dead body of the mother, into his captain's face, and then down at the baby, head now pressed against his breast.

'Speak,' encouraged Guy, after a pause as he noticed the expression. 'Thou hast been wondrous gallant, Thayendanegea; I will grant thee thy wish.'

The lad's face glowed, but he dropped into the Mohawk

tongue as a better medium for his expression. 'May I take her back to my Lady Catherine?' he asked.

Guy Johnson stared. 'Why dost wish to do that, Thayendanegea?' and the answer came readily.

'That she may teach her—as she is teaching me. That some day this little one may help me lift my people as we are being lifted up.'

Who could refuse a plea expressed like that? Certainly not Guy Johnson, and when the cavalcade returned to Johnson Hall, Thayendanegea, weary yet triumphant, bore a sleeping baby in front of him upon the piebald pony and, having paid respect to his gratified patron, turned to the Lady Catherine and placed the baby in her arms.

Of course she was surprised, but a few words from Guy Johnson explained, and also in broken accents the Indian added his plea. Sir William, who had planned to announce the formal engagement of his daughter and his nephew, listened in some surprise, but offered no objection when Catherine in a few kindly words consented to take charge of the little one and bring her up in her own household.

'We will have her baptized, Thayendanegea,' she continued. 'Our Reverend Doctor Stewart will receive her into the Christian Church, and thou shalt name her what thou wilt.'

The boy's face glowed. 'Then let it be thy name,' he said shyly, 'for as the moonlight is to this dark earth, so art thou to me.'

It was at this point that Sir William Johnson laid his kind hand on the brown shoulder. 'And what can I do for thee, Thayendanegea? Thou hast proved thyself right gallant, and I am proud.'

The lad paused, drew himself erect, and then answered slowly, but in excellent English. 'Thou canst redeem thy promise, Sir William. Let me learn how I may lift my people; send me to school.'

The great soldier laughed. He had almost forgotten the incident of that June day, though a glance at the tell-tale gashes on the balustrade reminded him; so while Mr. Stewart stood by, an interested listener, Guy and Catherine took up the lad's plea and urged Sir William's consent.

It was evident he had not considered the matter seriously, however, though he listened good-humouredly enough, and frankly recalled his promise. Then he turned to the lad.

'I do remember now,' he said crisply, 'that I made a stipulation. It was if thou couldst read to me one chapter of a book I gave to thee. Well?'

Thayendanegea glanced at Catherine, and at a quiet nod from her produced the book.

'I am ready to read it now, sir,' he said.

Sir William sat upright and stared, a smothered exclamation rippled through the room, but at another nod from his patroness, the boy opened the book and read aloud in clear, unfaltering tones:

'"In those days the multitude being very great, and having nothing to eat, Jesus called His disciples unto Him, and saith unto them, I have compassion——"' then lifting his eyes to his patron's, he said softly:

'This begins the eighth chapter of St. Mark's Gospel of the Lord Jesus Christ, sir. Shall I go on?'

'Yes.' Sir William answered in a low voice, and the reader continued:

'"I have compassion on the multitude because they

have now been with Me three days and have nothing to eat." '

On went the faithful voice, faltering scarcely at all, from verse to verse of that so wondrous story, while the listeners stood silent, wide eyes travelling from the motionless Sir William to that slim boy, and back again.

' " For what shall it profit a man, if he gain the whole world and lose his soul? Or what shall a man give in exchange for his soul? " '

' That will do.' Sir William rose, his voice strangely husky, and placed a hand on the wild head, then reverently bent down. ' Thy desire is granted, Thayendanegea. Dr. Stewart, when thy school re-opens this fall, take this new pupil along with thee, and teach him well, for me.'

' Gladly,' returned the good cleric, whose emotion was visible, ' and I will be thy friend, as well as thy teacher, O Thay—Thay—— '

' One suggestion only do I make,' interposed Sir William. ' Thy name, though dignified, is passing difficult as thou canst hear, for a white man's tongue. As thou dost aspire to be friend, mediator, interpreter between thy race and mine, adopt a white man's name.'

The Indian remained grave for an instant and again his glance sought the face of Lady Catherine. Again she nodded, and the boy replied at once.

' I will. Let me be called Joseph Brant, and grant that this reverend teacher may baptize me, even as he doth this poor baby, into the Christian faith.'

So it happened the very next day, when the afternoon lights grew long and golden, that a reverent group assembled in the long drawing-room of Johnson Hall. Sir William was present, with his daughter on his arm, and beside her

Captain Guy. A kindly looking woman was holding the little one, and nearby stood one or two trusted men-at-arms, while Sergeant Jenks was stationed near the door. Briefly and reverently the Indian child was christened ' Catherine ', and the surname added was ' Tourturelle ', which as Catherine whispered to her lover, is the French translation of Turtle, the poor child's family name. But Thayendanegea scarcely heeded all this. In his heart glowed a joy, deep and triumphant. In his ears were still echoes of the wise admonitions the kind cleric had uttered when they talked together alone that morning. Presently, at a sign from his protectress, he stepped forward and knelt before the clergyman at an improvised altar. The service continued—the prayers, the questions—and then he felt the waters of baptism upon his forehead, saw the hand uplifted in benediction, and heard the quiet words pronounced : ' Joseph Brant, I baptize thee in the Name of the Father and of the Son and of the Holy Ghost, Amen.'

CHAPTER IV

It was high summer time again at Johnson Hall, and an air of bustle and expectancy pervaded the whole establishment. From the Grist Mill beyond the quarters of Sir William's staff echoed the rumble of ox-carts and the clatter of hooves mingling with the rhythmic tumbling of the wheel, and from the quarters themselves arose the hum of activity. Even the soldiers stationed near the blockhouses and at the rear of the building seemed unusually active, though it was apparently no threat of hostility that inspired them. Rather an atmosphere of triumphant tranquillity pervaded the place, mingled with jovial anticipation that affected officer and man.

Ten years had passed away since that late August afternoon when Sir William Johnson had introduced his new pupil to Dr. Stewart. Ten years during which, despite the irksome discipline and necessary confinement, which fretted a nature such as his, Joseph Brant studied faithfully and well. Even six months made a difference, as Sir William discovered when he paid a flying visit to the school, for the boy was then able to converse fluently in English and read, write, and cipher in a way that delighted the scholarly soldier. What pleased him more, however, was the master's account of the lad's sincere religious inclinations; the old superstitions and fears of his race seemed fading from a mind daily becoming more intelligent and alert. The following summer, when the boy returned briefly to Johnson Hall to be present at the marriage of Captain Guy and Catherine Johnson, all his friends were delighted with his progress, for he had added to his studies not only the mastery of the mother tongue, but also other languages such as French and Greek. It was during this visit that he confided to the Lady Catherine his secret ambition, namely, to translate the Bible, or a portion of it, into his own Mohawk language, so that, as he said in his slow, musical English, ' Mine own people, ignorant children of the forests though they be, may get some chance to turn their faces toward the light.'

Some three years later, he left school and returned to reside at Johnson Hall, where Sir William made him his private secretary, and used him much in the administration of Indian Affairs, and so came the time when the Indian lad's early ambition was achieved, for now he had access to all the books in Sir William's library, and many were the leisure hours he spent absorbed in their contents. Captain Johnson and his lady had an establishment of their own twelve miles distant, for during the brief periods of peace Guy was also occupied with his uncle's work, but Catherine, even when she had children of her own, did not neglect affairs at Johnson Hall, and at least once a month prepared to spend a few days there. Little Kate Tourturelle, however, remained in seclusion, growing, as her adopted mother affectionately declared, ' prettier and more intelligent every day ', yet Catherine's wise control subjected her to firm though kind discipline, which served her well as a leader of her people's womanhood later on.

The outbreak of the Pontiac Wars called Joseph Brant abruptly away from his peaceful pursuits. He went with reluctance, for at that time he was planning to collaborate with Doctor Stewart, his teacher, who had now retired as schoolmaster, but still remained as missionary to the Mohawks. Together they were translating the Book of Common Prayer, and planning more extensive work. But song and story as well as history have preserved accounts of this, for the gallant boy was developing into splendid manhood, brave, clever, forbearing. One observer wrote of him that ' He behaved so like the Christian and the soldier that he gained great esteem ', and now it was common knowledge that this sincere Indian student soldier desired, more than anything else, to lift his humbler brethren and make them good.

Brant was of a modest disposition, and scrupulously honest even concerning himself. This became apparent in the account he wrote to his friend, Dr. Stewart, concerning the first pitched battle he was ever in. ' This being the first action in which I was present,' he said, ' I was seized with such a tremor when the firing began, I was obliged to take hold of a small sapling to steady myself; but after the discharge of a few volleys I recovered the use of my limbs and the composure of my mind, so as to support the character of a brave man, of which I was especially ambitious.'

Smilingly, Dr. Stewart had shown this naïve confession to Sir William, who slapped his knee, exclaimed admiringly, then told it to his daughter and son-in-law, and together these three watched with pride the splendid dawn of a nature that betokened no man of common breed, but a prince among his own.

It was during this long campaign that Joseph Brant received the British title of Captain, and thus was recognized no longer as the protégé at an Indian Charity School, but a cultured gentleman, trusted officer of His Britannic Majesty's armies of North America. This was the reason for so much joyous preparation at Johnson Hall, for it was with these honours now upon him that he was returning there, after an absence of perhaps four years.

'Arrah, thin! Come up wid ye, lazibones!' roared Sergeant Jenks, a little more grizzled than of yore, but lusty and alert, and he prodded a young recruit, half Indian, half French, in the midriff, and pulled him to his feet with no gentle hand. 'It's elber grease an' perseverance ye're wantin' on that bridle-bit, me son, not a snooze in the sun. An' if Captain Brant can't see his face in the side o' that saddle, it's confined to barracks ye'll be, I'm thinkin' an' sarves ye right!'

'Why so,—he like me—Indian,' returned the other morosely.

'Is he so?' snorted the Sergeant, disapproving gaze on the delinquent. 'Thin, shurean' faith, an' ut's niver since Oi left Ould Oireland that Oi iver did see two likes more different! Git a polish on that bit, ye spalpeen, or its' yer hide I'll be shining instead!'

So it was all through the Hall, bustle, activity, delighted anticipation, as of a proud family welcoming home their hero son.

'Kate, my dear,' remarked sensible Catherine to the slim, shapely maid who attended her. 'Methinks now thou art so tall, thy hair should be braided, not left floating loose, like a hoyden miss from the nursery. And see here, I have a ruby gown for thee of more decorous length—the better to hide thy somewhat lanky legs.'

The girl looked up, a shadow crossing her sensitive face, which, before she could hide, her mistress noted.

'Nay, shrink not, child,' she said kindly, 'I meant not to hurt thee.'

'Am I—am I so very ugly?' asked the girl, speaking

perfect English, but with the customary slow, soft drawl.

'Ugly? Why no, thou art merely at the "growing stage". The probability is that thou wilt be most beautiful, but a few years hence. Then I will curl thine hair, and build it high as the ladies of Old London and France wear theirs, and thy gowns shall rustle and sweep the floor as thou seest mine. But for the present, dress as I bid thee, and braid thine hair.'

'He—he will think I am but an Indian,' sighed the girl.

'He? Who? Captain Brant meanest thou?'

'Y-yes, my lady.'

'Ah, yes. The little babe he carried back upon his breast from her dead mother's arms is sure to win a special smile from him. But as for thinking thee an Indian, well, is he not one himself?'

'Did he carry me on his breast?' murmured the girl, unheeding the last remark, 'close there?'

'Ay, with thy little head pillowed beneath his chin, for sound asleep thou wert when he bent from his saddle, and so thou didst glide, all unconsciously, from his encircling arms into mine.'

The girl looked up adoringly, as her mistress continued. 'But, why this—this hero-worship? I hardly knew that thou hadst seen him since.'

'I did once, my lady, when he paused briefly before the gateway of our home, ere he rode to the Pontiac Wars.'

'That is well over three years ago,' said Catherine. 'And thou wert smaller, much. Well, now he shall see thee again, no longer a child, but growing fast to maidenhood.'

'But he did not see me then,' returned Kate, half mischievously, 'I hid myself, and watched him.'

'What? Coy, wert thou? He would have joyed in his protégé then, for his heart is as tender as it is brave. Never mind, he shall see thee now, and be more proud of thee for the promise of thy womanhood. And yet,' here she paused with a half-laugh, 'I do mis-doubt me if he will see aught save the face of his Chosen.'

'His—his what, my lady?'

'His chosen bride, my Kate. Moon-Bow of the Oneidas. Didst not know that he plans to marry the daughter of their Chief? It is part of my father's plan to honour him, this grand welcome and celebration for the marriage of Captain Brant and Moon-Bow. I do admit 'twas somewhat of a surprise for us all, but I hear she is very lovely. Now haste thee! 'Tis almost time for the Captain's arrival, and he may bring other guests. Hand to me that sky-blue poplin, child, and, look you, bathe and groom thyself with care, and put on that ruby gown I placed for thee upon my bed, and remember, braid thy hair.'

So saying, and with many more last minute directions, lovely Catherine Johnson hurried over her own preparations and hastened from the room.

Left alone, the Indian girl looked briefly at the pretty, suitable gown her mistress' kind care had provided, then slowly departed into her own inner room, untied the band encircling her hair, and slipped out of her dress. Then she returned to the room, her rich hair hanging in disorder about her arms and shoulders, and stared long and critically into the mirror there.

What she saw was a face glowing rose under palest gold, a little thin, perhaps and with cheek bones prominent, but with well-defined features, and promise of a softened contour later on. Arms, neck, and shoulders also a little spare,

but with the same promise of shapeliness, and these shrouded
in a wealth of thick, black hair which constant brushing
had made to glow like the proverbial raven's wing. The
mouth was grave, for so young a girl, yet sweet, and the
chin very resolute, and all this was lit by a pair of large, dark
intelligent eyes, clear, and very beautiful.

Long and thoughtfully the girl stared at herself, not
with any motive of cheap conceit, but apparently familiariz-
ing herself with herself and considering herself point by
point. Then she murmured beneath her breath : ' I wonder
if she is more beautiful than I can ever be ! '

Just then lively voices without startled her. She returned
hastily to her own, cubicle-like room, and proceeded to
array herself as her mistress had desired.

In the grounds below all was excitement. The friendly
tribes and sub-tribes, the Mohawks, the Oneidas, the Turtles,
and many others were gathered within that belt of trees,
commonly known as the Council Ground, that park-like
stretch of land, containing the well and overlooked by the
windows of the Hall. Often the Indians gathered here to
confer with their loved Superintendent, and that he should
have invited them, with a ceremony almost amounting to a
Royal Command, to be present at the home-coming and
marriage of his loved ' blood brother ', Thayendanegea,
now one of their recognized leaders, moved even their stoic
natures to delight. Camp fires were blazing, the feast pre-
paring, groups of ceremonial dancers and other performers
all arranged in readiness for the time when the young
Chief's cavalcade should appear. Just as Catherine arrived
on the steps of the main entrance, distant shouts and hurrying
figures told her that the guest of honour was arriving, and so,
flanked by her husband and her father, she too looked out

with eagerness and not a little curiosity for the first appearance of one who went forth a half-tamed savage, to return a cultured gentleman, and trusted officer of the British Crown.

Captain Joseph Brant was at this time about three and twenty years of age. Stories of his fame and chivalrous behaviour were current among friend and foe, and had even been relayed across the ocean, as also were admiring comments concerning his person. Therefore did Catherine look for much, nor was she disappointed when the central figure of all this rejoicing came in view. He was a tall man now, erect and stately, bearing, though with unconscious grace, an air of command. Hawk-like of face, firm of mouth, yet with eyes that were strangely wise and kind, though searching and observant. As Catherine watched him, astride his massive chestnut charger, which he managed with such easy grace, her mind took a swift flight to that other time when a ragged, wild-haired figure, astride a shaggy piebald pony, had approached. She whispered to her husband: 'La! But he is vastly changed! Put this man in a suit of ancient armour and we have before us a scion of England's knighthood.'

Thayendanegea's dress and accoutrements were in keeping with his person. A feathered crest surmounted the stately head, the encircling band richly adorned with beadwork, and while his nether garments were conventional breeches and leggings of very fine blue cloth, also elegantly trimmed with beads, his military coat was green, with silver epaulets, and lacing of silver. Across his saddle was a blanket of warm blue cloth striped with red, and by his side hung a superfine steel cutlass also mounted in silver and set with flashing gems.

D

He presented a gorgeous figure, and carried his trappings so well that neither he nor his wildly acclaiming followers appeared theatrical or overdone. An air of gentlemanly restraint pervaded the whole personality of the man, and just now it was tempered with another emotion, for by his side, mounted on a pretty white and brown gelding, rode Moon-Bow, of the Oneidas, Thayendanegea's chosen bride.

The cavalcade paused at the steps, the young Chieftain leaped from his saddle, strode up to them, then dropping on one knee before beautiful Catherine, took her hand and pressed it to his lips. If a page from the Age of Chivalry had suddenly turned back, the action could not have been more gracefully or spontaneously done, nor his words as he addressed her, better chosen or pronounced.

'Greetings to thee, my dear lady, my patroness. Truly my heart has longed for this moment, that I might thank thee with all my humble soul! Think of me not as a warrior, nor any great Chief, but just as thine humble pupil and servitor, for such I shall be while my life shall last.'

'Rise, Thayendanegea,' returned Catherine, responding instantly to his courtliness. 'Thine appearance and thy renown are my reward; thy friendship is my precious privilege!'

'Then know me by mine English name,' he pleaded. ''Twas thy kind heart that made me love that, too.'

He offered his arm, like a courtier of Old France, and Catherine, her hand resting lightly upon it, led him towards the two gentlemen. Greetings between them were less formal, for Guy Johnson, now a Colonel, had until recently been with him in the campaign, and Sir William had only withdrawn a few months earlier, on account of failing health.

They were proud of him, however, and greeted him heartily, and then the young Chief turned again and led Catherine down the steps.

'As thou didst receive me, now so long ago,' he said, his musical tones acquiring a pleading note, 'So I do pray thee, receive my heart's beloved. As I would wed her by the sacred rites of the Christian Church, so I would have her shy, sweet nature glorified by thy strong, tender one.' Then lifting the girl from the saddle, he led her forward. 'My loved Lady Catherine, receive Moon-Bow, of the Oneidas, my promised bride.'

The lady's two hands were extended in spontaneous and kindly greeting. Then he put his arm around the girl, his stately head bent protectively above her, and led her to the others.

Guy Johnson, even amid the celebrations that followed, had time for observation, and had found something to perplex him. He alone had seen the faint cloud on his wife's white brow, when she met the young bride, he alone had caught a sigh, not unlike regret. He was surprised, for the marriage seemed very suitable. Moon-Bow was a princess of the proud though tractable Oneidas, and was of the highest type of Indian beauty. Small and slight she was, with a wealth of thick black hair, large liquid eyes, and sweet regular features. He noticed her hands seemed unusually fragile and fluttery for an Indian maid's, and when she spoke, which was in broken English, her words were often punctuated with a slight cough.

'Nervousness,' he thought. 'She is but a forest child, and all this excitement is bewildering her.' Yet somehow this explanation did not seem to satisfy, and he glanced again at Catherine, but her face was calm and impassive now, as she led the pretty girl through the great doors and up the main stairway. There was little time for preparation, for the ceremonies began almost at once; a native celebration first, and then, by insistence of Chief Brant, a sacred ceremony in the Hall's private chapel.

Soon all was in readiness. Moon-Bow appeared again, with Catherine beside her, and in the excitement few noticed the red-clad silent girl with the heavy braids of hair who walked a pace or two behind. Soon the elaborate ceremonies, presided over by the principal Chiefs were in progress, but Guy noticed again that, when the ceremonial pipe was passed to her, Moon-Bow started to cough as soon as she put it to her lips. Catherine was near, however, and at a word from her, the watching Kate produced a glass of water, and the incident passed. Again, Guy noticed that pucker on his wife's brow, that suggested regret, but it passed immediately, and, the native ceremony concluded, the procession re-formed, and they all repaired to the Chapel, where Dr. Stewart, the missionary, was awaiting them. Now the bride was standing before the altar, her stately bridegroom beside her, and she made a pretty figure, clad as she was in white beaded doeskin, heavily fringed, her feet shod in moccasins that glistened in silver and blue. She uttered her responses clearly and intelligently and the deep earnestness of Joseph Brant's replies left no doubt as to what was in his heart. So the kindly cleric handfasted the couple ' by giving and receiving of a ring ', and pronounced them ' man and wife in the sight of God and those present assembled ' ; and as he pronounced the solemn closing words, ' Whom God hath joined let no man put asunder ', the stately Chief of the Mohawks, with a strong, yet gentle clasp, drew the beautiful Moon-Bow to his breast.

More celebrations were to follow. Sir William had given a banquet in the long, richly furnished dining-room, and he sat with bride and bridegroom on either side of him, his guests of honour. Later, as evening dropped into night, and the wedding party set off again to Chief Brant's fine residence, Canajoharie Castle, some few miles away, it was Colonel Guy and his lady who stood on the steps of the Hall watching the last of the company pass from view. Then as the Colonel turned, he noticed again on Catherine's brow that same faint pucker of distress.

' What ails thee, sweetheart, art tired? ' he asked affectionately, drawing her arm through his.

' N-n-no,—that is, yes. Wilt walk with me, Guy, a little while in our old rose garden? ' she asked, hesitating a second, then speaking with sudden decision.

' With pleasure, love. Methinks of all fair spots on earth that is to us the fairest,' he answered promptly.

Such a speech would ordinarily have brought a smile to Catherine's lips, for, wife and mother though she was of some years standing now, her husband was to her a lover still. She glanced at him affectionately, but her face remained grave, and she said nothing till they reached the well-remembered seat on the rock, where peaceful moonlit dusk brooded over sleeping mill and purling brook.

' Guy, I am troubled.'

' So I see, my dear. What is the matter? '

' This—this marriage, it—— ' Catherine paused as if at a loss for words, and her husband regarded her in surprise.

' What, Captain Brant and his lady?   Surely thou dost not disapprove of it? '

' I—I'm not at ease, Guy.'

' But, why, dear love?   Can anyone doubt that he loves her dearly or that she—— '

' Loves him,' supplemented Catherine.   ' N-no, I suppose not.   It's not exactly that, it is—it is—Oh!   I don't know what it is, but I wish—wish—— '

' Come, my Catherine, what is it that you wish? ' urged Colonel Guy, surprised at her apparent uncertainty and unease.

' That she were—altogether a little more—robust.' Catherine brought out the word with a rush, as if she had been mentally casting around for and had only just discovered one that suited.   Then, not waiting for his comment, she suddenly asked :

' Hast seen small Kate—our Kate, during these long hours of festivity? '

' Not recently,' he answered.   ' When thou wast arraying Moon-Bow for her bridal, she came to greet me, and I presented her to her preserver, Chief Brant.'

' By name? ' asked Catherine, and he nodded.

' Yes.   I told him here was baby Kate, grown tall and long-legged, but still remembering that she owed her life to him.'

' Thou—H'm!   What did he say? '   That the lady intended to say something else, then checked herself, was obvious, but he scarcely heeded and went on :

' Say?   He?   Why, I hardly remember, there was much going on as thou dost know.   As I think he patted her head, and told her to be a good girl, and mind what her mistress—that's yourself, my Cathie, commanded! '   and

Colonel Guy yawned lazily, and leaned back, hands behind
his head.

' He—patted her head? ' repeated his lady, staring straight
before her.

' Yes.'

' Said he aught else? '

' Why, n-no, nought I can recall. You know, Cathie,
when a man's attending his own wedding he's not likely
to notice any other female, young or old. Indeed, in
the circumstances I do bethink me that thou wert highly
favoured.'

Still Catherine did not smile; instead she went on:

' Canst remember if he—looked at her? '

' Why, no—I cannot; not intently anyway. But
Catherine, my own, why all these strange questions? '

She made no answer, and presently she rose. ' Come, let
us go in, Guy. It has been a great day, and I must find my
little maid.'

She hurried somewhat down the garden path, and Guy
strode beside her, wondering. A call from his father-in-
law attracted him as they entered the Hall, and stepping
aside he joined that gentleman, while Catherine went on
thoughtfully to her room. It was dark when she entered,
though moonbeams were throwing fitful glances on the
tables, the dressing glass, the huge four-poster bed. It was
at the foot of this bed that Catherine paused with a start,
though with little real surprise; then she stooped and
suddenly gathered a crumpled, woe-begone figure into her
arms. It was little Kate, tear-stained and tumbled, the pretty
new red dress but a crumpled thing, and she was sobbing as
though her heart would break.

Just then Catherine did not question her; she seemed to

understand, and she drew the quivering, grieving form into her own kind arms, and held her closely till the storm had spent itself; nor did she look surprised or even question when low words came, muttered at first, then uttered clearly over and over again:

'He wouldn't wait for me. . . . Oh! Oh! . . . He wouldn't wait, he wouldn't wait—for me!'

CHAPTER V

THE Dominion of Canada numbers, among even its present population, families who possess the privilege of writing U.E.L. after their names, and those letters signify as proud a heritage, as noble and heroic an ancestral record as any traced from Charlemagne or The Conqueror. The right to so use those letters can be claimed alone by those Canadians whose forefathers braved danger, disease, loss, imprisonment, and death for the sake of the United Empire they loved, the possibilities of which they had even then the vision to discern. Not that they obstinately proclaimed her right in everything—history has recorded the American War of Independence to be in claims and cause justified, whatever the methods of attainment might be, and as for the hardships and indignities inflicted by both sides upon each other, the mutual regret and condemnation by other sides, in this better age, speaks for itself. ' We were too much alike '; so declared one who tried to explain it all, ' and so it was best that we should go our separate ways apart, but not afar ', and it was about this time in Joseph Brant's career that the American Colonies declared their independence, and those long years of struggle, reprisal, and revenge began.

The storm had rumbled for a long time. Obstinate stupidity at home, resentful defiance at hand, smouldered in indecision, and then burst, isolated incidents here and there, small in themselves, helping to precipitate the crash.

Echoes of disturbance had reached the Johnson mansion, and Sir William, despite failing health, energetically employed his nephew and his ' blood-brother ', Chief Brant, to keep order throughout the portion of the country for which he was responsible. Not much enforcement was necessary, for the Indian Tribes were very content with the wise, sympathetic administration of their Superintendent, and were inclined for peace, though they watched with consternation and dismay the gathering dissatisfaction between sections of their White rulers which was rapidly dividing them into warring factions. Joseph might have shared in the perplexity but for the thorough ground-work of his education which taught him to consider carefully even the hidden things, ere he judged. Frequent conversations with Sir William and his now dear friend, Colonel Guy, made him master of the situation. A help, too, were the object lessons he discovered among the Six Nations themselves, whose Chief, Little Abraham, was far from co-operative, and whose pronouncedly retrogressive attitude caused unrest even among that hitherto united group.

Brant had discussed matters long and often with Colonel Guy, and because of that gentleman's fair-minded attitude towards the Revolutionists, Brant declared himself in agreement, and that come what may, he would ' sink or swim with the British '—a vow that was to make his name immortal in his Empire's Hall of Fame.

He hurried to his own people, even then the coveted objective of the enemy, and by the sheer weight of his personality as well as by the subtlety of his oratory, induced that Confederacy to stand for King George. Overjoyed at this success in which the Mohawks, the Senecas, the Cayugas, Tuscaroras, and Onondagas were so whole-hearted, he scarcely heeded the somewhat reluctant attitude of the Oneida Chief—his wife's brother—nor the almost resentful attitude of Chief Little Abraham, whose forefathers had held the rank of Principal Chief of the Confederacy of the Six Nations for many decades now.

On his return to Johnson Hall, whatever doubts might have arisen in retrospection, were dispelled by the distress he found there. Kindly Sir William, worn out with long years of willing devotion and work, and distressed by the signs of gathering national storm, was failing fast. One morning, soon after the young Chief's return, he collapsed in his study, quite suddenly, and died. Matters were at such a pass then that prolonged or dignified mourning was impossible; hastily the staunch old Briton was laid to rest, and then, at the urgent plea of Chief Brant and a number of loyal Indians who were with him, Colonel Guy and Lady Catherine Johnson abandoned Johnson Hall, taking with them their servants and as many goods as they could collect, and travelled north, intent on reaching the safe shelter of fortified Montreal.

They acted not a day too soon. Already an expedition was sent out with orders to capture Colonel Guy Johnson, alive, if possible, but they had reckoned without the loyalty of Chief Brant and his skill in woodcraft. Colonel Guy and his party reached Montreal, though they failed on the way to organize a sufficient force with which to capture the Mohawk Valley, now definitely in the hands of the Revolutionists. Events moved rapidly for those leisurely days, and it was then that Sir Guy Carleton, Governor of Quebec, joined with Colonel Johnson in urging that Brant depart with that gentleman for England, where, as the ablest and most astute member of the Six Nations, he could in person plead their cause, and tell their story to the Imperial Government.

Who shall gauge then what pride of heritage swelled in the heart of this forest prince? He, Thayendanegea, son of Tehowaghwengaraghkin, fifth of the Sachems who bowed before the British Throne, into whose hands the Great White Queen had given the precious silver cups of the Communion, and a copy of the Holy Writ; he, Chief Joseph Brant, was chosen for this! Colonel Guy, sensitive to his friend's reaction, encouraged him, agreeing whole-heartedly with the project, and so, having seen Lady Cathe-rine and her household established in the comfortable security of Montreal, when the autumn season swung round again, Joseph Brant and his companion set sail.

An ocean voyage in those days was at best a long and tedious undertaking, and to one of Brant's free nature it was likely to prove very wearying. So indeed thought one of the spectators who watched the graceful ship glide down the river towards the City of Quebec and the Gulf. It was the Lady Catherine, and sad as she felt at the prospect of so long a separation from her own husband, she under-took the task of comforting the depressed Moon-Bow, who was to reside in the Johnson home. The English lady was clasping her now, round her waist, endeavouring by kind words to encourage her to look up and wave God-speed as the ship passed from view.

'Arouse thee then!' she urged, playfully rallying her. 'What! Must so great a Chief as he go out on so great an adventure without the added benediction of his wife's farewell?'

But Moon-Bow's head only bent the lower, and her thin body shook with muffled sobs. Lady Catherine remained patient and steadfast in her endeavours at comfort. She was really concerned by the other's fragility and the all-too-

frequent cough, and more than once she glanced over the
drooping head to where young Kate of the Turtles stood,
straight and lissom as a mountain pine, large, clear, dark
eyes scanning the bend of the river where the ship had all but
disappeared.

' There, they are gone,' she announced suddenly, then to
the other girl, ' Nay, sweet sister, weep not so. The days
will fly—they always do, so will the weeks and months.
Soon thou wilt be mounting this hill again with our loved
Lady Catherine and myself, and thou wilt see a brave ship
coming back again with thy loved Chief aboard ! '

' Laden with honours and prouder than when he left,'
supplemented Lady Catherine, glancing at the girl approvingly. ' Come, Moon-Bow, weep no more. Do as my
good Kate adviseth thee, take her arm, and mine and let
us walk down the wooded slopes together ! '

Moon-Bow did try to respond. In a little while she
seemed able to look up and smile, and then to talk a little.
But ever and anon that cough broke in to distress her, and
again that cloud of worry shadowed Lady Catherine's fair
brow, and Kate glanced from one to the other with a face
unusually grave.

When once more at home, though the Lady Catherine
would fain have been alone a little while, she felt that
Moon-Bow needed her, and so her guest and her household
duties occupied her until nightfall, when she sought out little
Kate.

Strangely enough the Indian maid seemed to have disappeared, and it was only after a long perplexed search, that
on passing through a secluded balcony, flower-screened, and
overlooking the river, Catherine thought she heard a
muffled sob. It came again, and again, and guided by the

sound, she came upon Kate, crouched behind a rustic seat, her head upon her knees, rich hair dishevelled over arms and shoulders and sobbing as if her heart would break.

' Why Kate ! My poor child, whatever—— '

' Oh my Lady, my Lady, I tried so hard to hide it from thee so that thou should'st never know ! '

' I should not know ? ' queried the lady sitting down and drawing the weeping girl towards her. ' What is it that I should not know ? '

There was silence, while keen blue eyes searched the tear-dimmed dark ones, which fluttered and lowered and fluttered again. Suddenly understanding came.

' Oh my poor little Kate, is it possible that thou lovest him—still ? '

The dark head bent lower, the slender gold-tinted hands covered a face where now the rich blood was mounting, and at last she whispered, ' Oh my Lady, dost thou think me so very wicked ?—For I do.'

The Lady Catherine was deeply distressed. Her sense of justice was too clear to urge her to condemn where she saw no sin. Yet prudence bade her be firm, for here was no time for temporizing. She paused a moment, then : ' His heart belongs most definitely to Moon-Bow, Kate—to whom he is married.'

' I know, I know, my Lady, and God bless her—always—always.'

' Oh my poor child, dost thou love him like that ? '

And the sweet sad face now steadily raised to hers had truth written upon it. ' Even so, my Lady, I do love him—like that ! '

' I had hoped—— ' began Catherine, then she checked

herself, concluding more slowly, ' —that it was but a child's fancy.'

To which the Indian girl answered just as quietly, ' And I am no longer—a child.' Then with a burst of honest distress. ' Oh my much loved Lady, dost thou think me very wicked?'

Catherine hesitated no more. She stooped, raised the girl from her knees, and drew her gently but firmly on to the seat beside her. Then with her own handkerchief she wiped the tear-stained face and smoothed the tumbled hair.

'Hear me now, Kate—nay, nay, hush thee—hush!— for I must talk with thee very seriously. There—there— that is better, be thy strong, sweet self. That is better— better still. Truly sayest thou, thou art no more a child, and an Indian princess chiefest of her tribe could not be more poised and royal than thou art. So—art better? Good, now hear me, for what I say to-night must be locked in our hearts for ever, to be mentioned no more between us, but to be remembered always. Art willing?'

And the girl, steady now, with eyes quiet and deep as hidden pools, answered promptly, ' I am ready and willing, my Lady.'

' Kate, from the time he brought thee to me, he a wild, half-savage himself—but thy life's preserver—I had hoped and dreamed that one day he might know thee for his own, and so claim thee. But it was not to be, his heart has wan- dered—elsewhere. That thou dost love him, little one, surpriseth me not at all, nor do I condemn a love so pure. Love, if it be true and unselfish minds only the welfare of the beloved, lives and prays and plans for that, minding itself not at all. It seeks not even to monopolize—nor even to possess, but it is content to worship from afar, in self-chosen loneliness, if by so doing the one beloved may be happy. True love makes of itself the very best, gives and is the very best, hoping by so doing that some day it may serve the one beloved. It defies fate, it defies pain, it is tireless, unquenched, yet for itself it asks nothing—sometimes not even for love returned. Tell me then, Kate—canst thou love him—like that?'

And the young girl answered steadily, 'Yea, my Lady, I both can—and do.'

The lady smiled, a light almost of triumph in her eyes. 'There speaks mine own true Kate, and I rejoice to hear thee. Courage, dear one—go on so loving him—for there is no sin in a love like that, and, though he knows it not now, he may need thy help some day, and need it desperately.'

'How? Oh my Lady! How?'

Quietly then, but concisely, the Lady Catherine told her adopted daughter the secret of Joseph Brant's ambition. How, as the splendid dawn of his own intellectual awakening grew to glorious day, he yearned to help his people to his knowledge also. How, with the collaboration of his friend and teacher Dr. Stewart, he had already begun the translation of the New Testament, into the Mohawk tongue, and how, when the days of strife were over, he longed to go back to that work again.

'. . . But he will need a woman's hand, my Kate,' continued the lady. 'No man, however clever he may be, can reach the heart of all his people always. Again, if the women are not taught—and the children—the mothers and fathers of the future, then is his work but half accomplished, and who hath he to teach them? Truly it is too great for one man to accomplish—so—dost understand now, my Kate?'

The girl did understand. Her eyes were bright and eager; then her face clouded. 'Moon-Bow,' she objected.

The Lady Catherine shook her head. 'The aid he will require can only be developed through years of preparation, profound study, thought, learning, and above all experience,' she said. 'Also his helper must possess a strong, stable mind, and a body robust that can sustain all this work.' Then, as the girl still seemed doubtful, she continued: 'Moon-Bow, even were she capable, is not physically strong enough. But he loves her,' she finished, quietly emphatic.

There was a longer silence now, then Kate threw back her head and rose to her goodly height. Lady Catherine gazed appreciatively at the tall young form, the proudly modelled throat, the noble brow, at the clear eyes and resolute, sweet lips. Then she smiled approvingly, as the girl said quietly, but very steadily: 'I do understand, my Lady. Tell me how I may best serve my people, for only in doing that can I hope to serve—him.'

'Thou hast spoken as I wished, my Kate, as befitting a princess of thy people, and mine adopted daughter. Yes,'— as the girl started, her eyes alight with pleasure and surprise— 'for thou art as a daughter to me now. Tell me, wilt enter a school that I will choose for thee, and learn all they have to teach thee, that some day thou mayst be a teacher too?'

And the Indian girl answered readily, 'Choose such a school for me, Mother Beloved. Choose well for me, and I will do my part.'

CHAPTER VI

A LONG ocean voyage in those days was a precarious business. Even with fair winds and weather one of such a length as Brant had undertaken could hardly be accomplished in less than six weeks, and should Atlantic gales break loose in but half their customary fury, it might be much longer. Fate was kind, however; the good ship made the crossing safely and with excellent speed. Autumn was far advanced before the green hills of England came into view, and Brant, who stood in the fore-part of the vessel, eager eyes strained towards the approaching shore-line, was sought hastily by Colonel Johnson, and urged to put on extra clothing as precaution against the damp November fogs.

'There is but slight mist,' he protested, laughing at his friend's insistence, yet submissively donning the many-caped greatcoat offered him, 'and I'll smother in this. Methinks that often over the crest of our Mount Royal I have seen a thicker veil, and colder, too.'

'But never more penetrating,' returned the Colonel. 'Have patience but a little while, my friend, and thou wilt see in truth that when the fogs of England settle down, it is literally impossible to see one's hand an arm's length away.'

Brant raised his eyebrows but said nothing, and presently the coast-line of England drew nearer till white cliffs were plainly visible, topped with crests of living green.

'Are those what I hear called "The White Walls"?' asked Brant, pointing to them, and his companion nodded.

' Yes. Dost remember in thy student days reading about " That pale, that white-faced shore, whose foot spurns back the ocean's rolling tide "? Well, there it is ! '

' It seems misty—and quite small,' observed Brant, after staring a while.

' Ay, it is. " A little body with a mighty heart ".' And then with a half-laugh, as if to conceal emotion, ' I' faith, at this season of the year, it is a wonder she is not wrapped in fog so thick that thou could'st not view her at all. Thou art fortunate, Chief Joseph; the Motherland is smiling to welcome her gallant Prince of the West."

Chief Brant's grave mouth relaxed slightly at the implied compliment; then he said, almost beneath his breath, ' And despite possession of my Golden Land of Promise, is it possible that ye can love this land best of all? '

' All her sons and daughters do—yes ! '

Brant stood silent, watching while the good ship ploughed her way up the Thames estuary, and after viewing the bare, brown fields on either hand, he said again, ' But why? As I know from my student days, it is a land but small, with a climate variable. Truly the drabness of this autumn landscape bears out that. Also it promises to be quickly overcrowded. There are other lands afar, vaster lands and richer ones—do we not both hail from such a one? Why must the great White Chief, whom I, with you, shall hail as " Majesty ", remain here? Why, of all the lands he rules and shall rule, must this drab-seeming England represent the core? '

' Drab it does seem at this time of year,' agreed Colonel Guy. ' Yet wait until spring appears again, and then—— But that is not the secret. Bethink thee, Joseph '; here he placed an affectionate hand on the other's shoulder. ' The body of a man, it is of goodly proportions, diversely shaped and capable of much. Yet is each portion responsible of individual performance, that is to say, the eyes see, the lungs breathe, and so forth, yet it is the heart that keeps vitality alight, and that by comparison is of itself small, and though accurately shaped—for a heart—is not as lovely to the eyes as the body's other parts. Is that not so?'

'And by that thou meanest——'

'Just that, Joseph. England, tiny, shapely, steady, is the heart of this great body, our growing Empire. Just so long as this heart remains healthy, steady, so shall the shapeliness of the mightier parts grow and be glorified. Let any taint come here in the core of our vitality, and our whole body, no matter how vast it be, shall wilt, become weakened, and in time, disintegrate.'

'God forbid!' ejaculated Joseph fervently, 'for the heart that can feel for and protect the weak is surely worth preserving.'

There was no time for more; the customary bustle of preparation for landing was all around them now. Colonel Johnson led Brant below and, with the methodical precision of a seasoned traveller, directed the gathering of belongings, and instructed the capable attendants who were to see to their transport. Then, in the conventional attire of English gentlemen, and wearing the now thoroughly appreciated greatcoat, Brant followed his friend up the deck, just in time to see the ship drawing near to the docks in London Pool.

Although he was not aware of it, the fame of this forest prince had gone before him, and when the gang-plank was lowered a group of stately gentlemen approached them. Colonel Johnson knew them for representatives of the best English society, the Duke of Devonshire, the Earl of War-

wick, and many others, and he had just time to whisper this
to his companion, and assure him that they were there,
emissaries from His Majesty, to bid him welcome, when
they were upon them, greeting them first with characteristic-
ally British formality, and with really genial warmth.

Brant was soon a favourite. The charm of his personality, his simple dignity and ease quickly impressed those
present, who were the flower of English chivalry, and by
the time they left the ship, and were riding in the Earl of
Warwick's carriage through the narrow streets of London,
all reserve had been discarded, and their main object was
to make their forest princeling happy, and his visit a success.

History has immortalized Joseph Brant's sojourn in
England. How, as the guest of the Earl of Warwick, he
met and received the noblest of the land. How his unaffected manner and simple but sincere piety won him
friends everywhere, and soon, though always under the
watchful eyes of his friend and companion, Colonel Johnson,
he was the honoured guest in a great many houses. That
was the age of elegance, of gallant men, of lovely women,
talented artists, great musicians and painters. Brant
bowed over the hand of the Duchess of Devonshire, listened
to the golden accents of the great actress Siddons, the sublime
music of the great master, Handel, who had died but a few
years before, and of course he sat to have his portrait painted
by that master of the brush and palette George Romney.

'Captain Brant,' said his host, the Earl, hurrying into his
room one day, 'It is my privilege to inform you that His
Majesty the King will receive you in audience at four
o'clock this afternoon. He commands your attendance,
and I am to conduct you thither.'

'There, think of that, Joseph lad!' exclaimed good-natured Colonel Guy, clapping him on the shoulder. 'The Great White Chief you dreamed of when you could scarce speak our tongue, hath sent for you that you may talk, man to man!'

'I—I shall attend His Majesty's pleasure,' answered the Chieftain, recovering from the confusion the sudden announcement caused. Then as friends old and new clustered around him, congratulating him, he asked gravely: 'How does one approach His Majesty, and how address him? Shall I fling mine arm aloft, in invocation of the Great Spirit, or shall I bow down upon my face?'

'Neither such extreme,' reassured Colonel Johnson amid laughter, and the Earl of Warwick added: 'It is usual to sink on one knee and gracefully kiss the King's hand.'

'Kiss his hand!' ejaculated Brant, genuinely astonished. 'But why? Methinks that were a foolish custom. Now if it were the Queen's hand, 'twould be another matter!'

More laughter greeted this remark, for it was uttered with genuine belief. Colonel Guy clapped him on the shoulder again, then slipped a kindly arm across the broad back. 'Be thine own, dignified self, Joseph,' he advised. 'A true man, bred in the heart of a young and growing country, a natural nobleman indeed, for whom the virgin forest was as castle and cathedral, whose books were Nature's growing things, and whose candles were the stars.'

So it came about that this little group of well-wishers ushered the gallant, yet simple-hearted prince of a younger world into the presence of the Majesty of England.

George III was at that time a man around forty. A personable-looking man, with kindly eyes and an understanding manner. Whatever his administration as a king, praised or blamed by history according to its verdict, as a personality he was, then, exceedingly popular. His manners were friendly and unaffected, and had earned him the sobriquet 'Farmer George', while his very real piety, which prompted him to religious expression and a blameless family life, was most commendable. In this matter he separated himself entirely from his Royal privilege, and was known to have reproved severely one sychophantic preacher who, upon the King's unlooked-for entrance into his church, changed his regular sermon and preached an unctuous and exceedingly flattering one for His Majesty's benefit. It had quite the opposite effect, however, for George declared afterwards, and with much heat, that he had gone there to hear the Divine Word and not to be toadied to!

Chief Joseph Brant entered the Royal presence in full Indian regalia, from elaborately feathered head-dress to finely wrought, elegantly adorned moccasins. By his side hung his steel tomahawk carved with the first letter of his Christian name, and his Mohawk appellation, Thayendane-gea. Truly he made a striking figure as he walked with unconscious grace towards where the King sat in a carved inlaid chair upon a low dais, and this King George evidently thought, for his eyes lighted and his composed features glowed with real interest, as he stretched out his hand towards his warrior subject. True to his instincts, the Western princeling did the right thing; he bowed over that majestic hand, then, stepping back respectfully, raised his hand, palm outward, in salute. 'From the green heart of my forest country I come to greet thee, O Great White Chief,' he said, speaking in the soft Mohawk dialect, 'From its great waters, its greater mountains, and its tameless winds and suns, it is thine, in its strength and its beauty, for I am come to lay it at thy feet.'

Colonel Johnson, who had accompanied the Red Indian prince into the presence of the King, translated promptly, and the King was evidently attracted by the address, especially as the manner in which it was rendered was unaffected and sincere. But he was still more gratified when, having paused to listen earnestly to the Royal words of welcome, Chief Brant spoke again, this time in perfect English :

' Your Majesty, it is scarcely in my simple capacity adequately to express my gratitude and loyalty for this so gracious audience.'

' It is we who have reason for gratification,' returned the King kindly, ' that our far-flung and growing realm can produce promise of such potency. It has been told to us, Chief Brant, that thou art loyal to our Crown.'

' With my limbs, my life and all my heart, O Majesty.'

' It is well, it is well,' replied the King, leaning back, keen eyes on the other's face. ' And thou dost speak not for thyself only, but for thy people, eh ? '

' Even as your Majesty speaks for us all,' returned the Chieftain, bowing again.

' Good ! They are a wise and warlike people, so we do hear,' said the King again, ' and even at this far distance we would prefer them as friends, not foes. Yet methinks we have heard tales of varying conduct. How accountest thou for this, Chief Brant ? '

' Much as your Majesty can personally account for all good or ill within thine own immediate realm,' returned Brant. ' People there, as here, are individually good or evil, wise or unwise, and react accordingly, Sire.'

The respectful fearlessness of the answer attracted the King. He gazed with frank admiration at the stately visitor, then said : ' We would know more of the people thou dost represent. Their wisdom, their customs, their forest lore—for instance, is it not claimed that they can tell from the trees and the wild animals what the weather will be ? '

A slight smile trembled on the grave lips of the Chief; then he answered respectfully :

' My people are but an awakening people, Sire; in many respects they are as children new roused to greet the dawn. Nature was their book of learning, and while they need to know much more, there are some things they understand. Truly the trees and the cloud-wrack tell them much, so do the corn husks, which before the coming of a long, cold winter will be thick, but if heralding a mild one, will be thin.'

' Amazing ! ' ejaculated the King, motioning him to go on, and Brant continued :

' When berries ripen twice in one season the wise ones declare the winter will be short, not here and there a meagre few, but spread out, plentiful, and red as the new harvest moon.'

These simple poetic utterances held the listeners enthralled, and the King said again, briefly, ' Go on.'

' It is true, your Majesty, that the wild things of the forest teach my brethren. The squirrels, when much cold is coming, seize and hoard all they can, but when winter is short and mild, they seem to know that, too, for many hickory nuts are left on the trees; they are not needed.'

Many more tales this son of the New World told his interested King, and the listeners almost forgot the customary formality in their eagerness to hear.

' And so, good Chief Brant,' said the King at last, ' ye

have come to plead the cause of thy people with us, as well
as to express their loyalty? Good. Now speak. What
wouldst thou have of us, for them?'

The Red Indian's face became grave; he drew his
stately form to its goodly height, then stretched out hands
that were in gesture almost pleading.

'The right, O Majesty,' he answered, 'the right to live
and to progress, even as our White brothers live. The
opportunity to teach them of the White Man's lore, and the
White Man's God. We, my people and I, have fought for
you, and for that sacrifice I pray grant us the right to live
and grow beside you now. We were promised our lands
for our services, and those lands we were to hold on the
same footing as those we fled from at the commencement
of the war, when we joined, fought, and bled in your cause.
Allow us, we pray, all privileges accorded to us as sovereigns
of the soil, which your Majesty's Government knows us to
be, your Majesty's loyal subjects, and against whom, provided that we are faithful, none other has any right tol
interfere.'

'For Heaven, thou pleadest eloquently!' exclaimed
George, rising to his feet. 'Nor shall it ever be declared
that the Majesty of England turned deaf ear to such. Thy
prayer is granted, Chief Brant. The Six Nations of the
Confederacy of Indians are free, free as my people of the
British Isles, to live, progress, and develop. Their lands
and property remain sacred to their use, and with only this
proviso: Whereas they are—as thou hast declared—forest
children but growing up into the wisdom of the world, so
shall they be the wards of our nation. The White Man shall
be their guardian and their protector, responsible for them
in all matters beyond their own comprehension; not to

impose restraint or persecute, in any unlawful manner, but to protect and advise. All this we do command our white subjects, under pain of our displeasure should they disobey. Go thy ways, Chief Brant, raise up thy people all thou canst, and be assured that in thy task, thy King is thy very good friend and well-wisher. In token of this, we do bid thee, for all thy life to come, that thou wilt wear this ring, to remind thee and all who know thee how George of England, as a king, appreciates a loyal subject, and as a man, admires another, and a very gallant one, too.'

So saying, His Majesty drew from his own finger a plain, but heavy, gold signet ring, and placed it on the Chieftain's hand.

'Have it engraved,' he said kindly, 'with thine own name, and wear it always as a memento of this interview and as a means of identification in life—or in death!'

So the audience ended.

CHAPTER VII

FROM that day forward, according to the common parlance of the times, Joseph Brant was a 'made man'. He became the popular guest of honour at most of the great houses of London; gifts were showered upon him, open admiration, and not a little flattery. Towards all, however, he bore himself with the same unspoiled dignity, unaffected by curiosity or adulation, childlike in his own eagerness to see and know all concerning the landmarks and historic sites around the old city, and he even travelled as far as the borders of Wales. Beneath the shadow of the ancient Tower he stood in awe. He strode through the grim old chambers, in and out of the haunted corridors, visited the awful dungeons beneath the fort's foundations, where many a State prisoner had sighed his life away in darkness and horror. Here only, he seemed affected and for a moment laid a heavy hand that shook slightly on Colonel Guy's shoulder ere he turned and hurriedly retraced his steps to the upper air. Then, at his friend's glance of inquiry, he muttered, 'I' faith, Johnson, even in her punishments thy nation exceedeth all others. Torture and the block could even I, savage that I was, defy, but to be shut up—beneath the ground—away from sound, or the sight of the blessed sun——! Ugh! Truly it must have been for some grievous fault that such cruelty was meted out as just reprisal.'

'Not always,' returned the Colonel with a sigh. 'There have been men, Joseph, innocent as thou or I, who have sobbed their lives away down here. Statecraft is a tricky game, my friend, and as individuals or as nations it is through strife, mistakes, and deep pain that we find our lost godhead—for lost it we most certainly have. Yet even this thou mayest turn to thy nation's advantage, Joseph, as may also the founders of the new nation in our awakening Canada. When thou dost essay to teach thy people, let the mistakes we made, when we were but growing, be to thee and all thy fellow teachers as landmarks, that the peoples may profit by our errors without the pain of making them.'

Soon after this they visited Westminster Abbey, and here, amid the dim aisles and sacred arches, Chief Brant was a different person. Gone was the arrogant, free step, the proud carriage of the princely head. He stood, hat in hand, shoulders bowed, humble, as he was conducted from shrine to shrine, from treasure to treasure, and was told what it all meant. On the threshold of Edward the Confessor's chapel he paused, while the history of that far-away monarch and his influence upon England was whispered to him, then suddenly, but with a simple sincerity that dispelled all suggestion of affectation, he dropped to his knees before the threshold, and for a while there was silence, and respectful waiting.

So the weeks of Chief Brant's visit rolled into months. Winter passed away, and spring began to come to England. Here it was that the nature-loving soul of the Red Man found his delight: the mist-like green that seemed first but breathed upon the land, developed into verdant glory; the starlike flowers of snowdrops pushed their gallant spearheads through the snow; the rain-washed woodlands; the whipping winds among mysterious lanes, deep-hedged and narrow.

It was about this time that the Prince of Wales, handsome dilettant that he was, conceived the idea of taking Chief Joseph among his own party and personally conducting him on a tour of what was the 'night life' of that day. Brant went willingly enough, for until then every visit to every new place had been one long story of interest and delight, but what he saw then was so different as to first bewilder and then to shock him. Colonel Guy, who was of the party, watched his friend with affectionate doubt, much perplexed concerning the best way of turning the Prince from his anything-but-admirable purpose. Thayendanegea, though he spoke little, was frank in expressing his opinions, and should his disgust get the better of him, he might not be particular about choosing diplomatic words wherewith to express it.

Nor was the climax long in coming, for after a few hours of such occupation, during which the Chief had been a silent but obviously unhappy spectator, he suddenly approached the heir apparent and bowed low.

'Think of me but as a wild man, your Highness,' he said gravely, and with just a tinge of sadness in his tones, 'or think that my still limited education has not yet reached the stage where this amuses me. Think what your Highness wills, yet never doubt my loyalty or respect for the Crown of your father, and having so done, let me withdraw.'

'Thou likest not this sort of amusement, eh, Chief Brant?' returned the Prince, striving to speak carelessly, yet avoiding, after a brief glance, the expression of shocked surprise in the warrior's eyes. 'This is a part of England thou admirest not—eh?'

'I repeat I am—or was but lately—a wild man, Highness.

I do know that some things which are not what they seem, are best to simulate what they are not; that is a White Man's law which, though I do not comprehend, I yet admit to have wisdom,' returned Brant, grave, direct gaze never wavering. 'And yet,' he continued—'and yet . . .'

'And yet what?' urged the Prince with a forced laugh, as the rest stood silent by. 'Come, speak thy mind; I will not be offended.'

Chief Joseph Brant drew himself to his goodly height. 'Sir, your Highness. Some day you will be a Great White Ruler of this land, of my land and others, maybe far-flung across the sea, and as the destined holder of such an heritage, forgive me when I say in honesty that this, and other such haunts as I have seen this night, seem very queer places for a Prince to go.'

'Thou mayest withdraw, Chief Brant,' returned the Prince briefly, a flush very like confusion on his own proud cheek. Then he nodded permission for Colonel Johnson to depart also, and added with the same careless air, 'But remember I shall expect to see thee at the grand masquerade at the Earl of Warwick's next week. It is given in thine honour, remember.'

'I shall not fail, your Highness,' returned the Chief with faultless courtesy; then he withdrew.

Dawn was breaking as they emerged into the narrow streets, and for some time they walked along in silence, Brant absorbed in his own thoughts, following tacitly where Colonel Johnson led. For some time their road followed the river bank, then a few twists and turns brought them beneath the frowning precincts of Newgate Gaol. 'This,' explained Johnson, in answer to Brant's look of inquiry, 'is where ordinary prisoners are confined, and often executed.'

' Executed? '

' Well, hanged, then. . . . Hullo! What's here? Oh,
it's the womenfolk of those two poachers who are to be
hanged this morning. I heard that execution was fixed
for dawn. The crowd will be all their friends and sym-
pathizers, I suppose—but who can that be with them? '

Familiarity had evidently made Colonel Guy more careless of the episode than his really kindly nature would
justify, but, before Brant could exclaim concerning it, the
attention of both was attracted to one person who stood amid
the sobbing group of women and children, and seemed to
dominate it like a strong tower. It was a little man in
black garments and with the white bands of the cleric.
Joseph Brant found himself staring at a grey head, a
sensitive face, with arresting features and fearless eyes. Just
then he was bending over a sobbing woman who knelt
in the dirt clinging to his coat. One hand was upon her
dishevelled head, and with the other he endeavoured to
raise her. Evidently he had been trying to speak words of
comfort to her and to them all, and between her incoherent
utterances and the sobs of her companions the new-comers
caught a word or two.

' —My Jim—my Jim—Mr. Wesley. Oh! sir, why will
they hang my Jim——? It was only a rabbit, Mr. Wesley—
a little, little rabbit—even if it was wrong to take it—isn't
my Jim worth more? Oh! Mr. Wesley, why will they
hang my Jim—for a rabbit? Jim was a good 'usband,
Mr. Wesley—a good father—Oh! who will look after the
children an' me now——? My Jim—my Jim—why will
they hang my Jim for a rabbit? Oh! Mr. Wesley, Mr.
Wesley—— ' and so on, over and over again.

Guy Johnson, with a muttered exclamation, took his

companion's arm and dragged him away. 'We can do nothing,' he said, sadly. 'Right or wrong, as we personally may regard the present laws, there is short shrift for poachers. 'Tis evidently that woman's husband, and he must hang to-day.'

'Do they hang men here for catching their food from the open fields?' gasped Brant, and the Colonel nodded shame-facedly.

'Alas, yes,' he said.

'But that woman, and her children, who will feed and clothe them?' protested the other, pulling against the compelling hand.

'God knows! Alas, and to England's shame be it admitted; there is much that she must cleanse herself of ere she prate with authority to her would-be sons abroad! Hark! Zounds, but the preacher chap is singing now!'

Into the sweet, clear air of the growing day a rich voice was rising, a baritone voice, guiding with honest emotion yet unwavering accents the faltering broken voices of the rest.

''Tis a prayer for their passing souls, belike,' whispered Johnson, pausing to look back. 'Hark! How that fellow can sing!'

The voice was rising strongly now:

> God is the refuge of His saints
> When storms of sharp distress invade;
> Ere we can utter our complaints,
> Behold Him present with His aid.
>
> Let mountains from their seats be hurled
> Down to the deep and buried there,
> Convulsions shake the solid world;
> Our faith shall never yield to fear!

F

'Who is he?' inquired the Indian Chief, as the full-throated melody continued :

> Zion enjoys her Monarch's love
> Secure against a threatening hour,
> Nor can her firm foundation move
> Built on His faithfulness and power!

and the Colonel answered :

'Wesley, John Wesley, itinerant preacher now, reformer some say, crank, say others. There are some who term him agitator, and others again who think of him as a Saint, or Apostle. He is a gentleman by birth and education, the son of a clergyman. But he has strange ideas; declares he is confined to no district, that the world is his parish where he may speak to all concerning the love of God. He is there in his capacity of comforter, I suppose, for the relations of those two poor fellows about to be strung up, and sure enough they need it! Maybe, and heartily I do hope it, this blundering though well-meaning England of ours will wake up to the enormity of such conditions! How the fellow can sing! Hi! Brant! Where are you off to?'

The clear, courageous voice had never faltered through all this hurried account, and now Brant turned suddenly as the hymn's last verse arose, the little group, despite their open agony, joining in bravely. Before the sound died away, and at a gesture from the cleric that little group sank to their knees, the tall Indian Chief stood right beside him, and was pushing a bag of money into his hand.

'For her,' he whispered, indicating the woman, and in answer to Wesley's surprised look : 'I can do nothing, but I am very sorry. Take it for her!'

Then he hurried away.

* * * * * *

It was the night of the grand masquerade, and the leading personalities of fame and fashion, arrayed in extravagant attire, were rolling up in their gilded coaches to the stately entrance of the Earl of Warwick's town house. Apart from the fact that it was one of the gala affairs of the now closing season, it possessed the added attraction of a real live Indian Chief as guest of honour, and so popular and colourful a figure was Brant by this time that speculation ran high as to what sort of costume he would choose to disguise himself, for his excellent knowledge of history laid several avenues of choice before him, and many amused themselves conjecturing how they could penetrate his disguise and discover him before the time of unmasking came.

In speech and bearing he was as a courtier born, but his bronzed skin and weather-beaten features might have been observed under any disguise, and for that very reason Brant had elected to adopt no disguise at all, but go in his full war regalia, his features merely heightened by war paint. As this was exactly what nobody expected him to do, for a long while his identity remained concealed, save to those few intimates who knew his secret, and much amusement did this doughty son of the Americas derive from the freely expressed speculation concerning his whereabouts, especially when he joined in the search himself. Even when unmasking time came he was not recognized, and by that time the ballroom and ante-chambers were hot to suffocation, and there were many who had feasted not wisely, but too well, and were regrettably excited with wine.

Chief Brant was an abstemious man. Long ago he had given a promise to Catherine Johnson that he would avoid intoxicating drink which spelt disaster to so many and positive ruin to his race, and despite the laxity of the times, both in his social and business life he managed to keep that promise. As it happened, he was one of the few sober men in that assembly then, and he was looking on at the frankly hilarious scene with somewhat mixed feelings, when an incident occurred which has now become history. One of the revellers, a young lordling with more pomade on his head than sense within, had amused himself, since being turned out of the gaming room, by trying to stare the Indian out of countenance. Of course he took him for a reveller like himself, but in a very good disguise, and after confusedly trying to identify him, was seized with that not rare desire among inebriates, to chastise him for some fancied wrong. So with many confused notions of offended dignity revolving in his poor, crazed head, and in less time than it takes to record it, he lurched forward, elbowed his way between Colonel Guy and another who were talking with Brant apart, seized the Indian by the nose, and pulled it vigorously!

The next instant the room was electrified by the most blood-curdling yell that ever issued from human lips! It was the deadly war-whoop of the Mohawks, and there in the middle of the company stood an awful figure of an Indian on the warpath, his paralysed victim flung to his knees and held by the hair, while around his head, up and down, this way and that, seeming to miss its mark by but a hair's breadth, flashed the Indian tomahawk!

There was a second of awful pause, then a universal shriek and a scuffling as many guests made for the exits; one or two jumped through the windows, and not a few hastily barricaded themselves behind overturned tables. Next instant they turned to stare again, and then to laugh with hysterical relief, for the furious figure of a moment ago had as suddenly stilled, the tomahawk returned harmless to the girdle, and stooping over the limp ' victim ', Chief Brant raised him to his feet, remarking courteously and in perfect English : ' I hope I have not frightened you too much.'

For the other guests the discovery only added to the gaiety of the evening, but the young lordling was completely sobered with the shock, and as he stared into the grimly smiling face of the man who held him, and stuttered out words appropriate to the *dénouement*, he felt he had lived ten years in those few seconds, and that, for him, life could never again be quite the same !

It was but a few weeks after this that Brant planned to depart for Canada. He had been showered with expressions of good will, with gifts, and invitations to return. What gratified him most was the possession of the written royal assent and confirmation of his position which was to materialize into the deed of gift from the Crown to the Six Nations, granting them that fertile strip of country in the heart of Upper Canada. Often he read it over, for its words were, to him, as music :

' . . . The said Mohawk Nation, and such of the Six Nations as wish to settle in that quarter to take possession of and settle upon the banks of the Ouse or Grand River, running into Lake Erie, allotting to them for that purpose, six miles deep on either side of the river, beginning at Lake Erie, and extending in that proportion to the head of the said river.'

More than all his personal honours Chief Brant prized this. It represented so much, a lifetime of patient endeavour and fidelity, and faith and perseverance in the face of official delay and sometimes, even downright dishonesty and neglect. It represented hard campaigns fought and won, losses sustained, and maybe material advantages denied. Everybody knew that Thayendanegea, with his brilliance and military skill, was the coveted prize of the Revolutionists; they tried to coax him with promise of honours and award to their side, and failing this, they tried to kill or capture him, but he eluded this last, and remained, even in the face of the most tempting offers, loyal to the British Crown.

Some well-earned reward was in sight now, however, and Colonel Johnson, watching over his friend through all these triumphs, shared with him his gratification and enthusiasm. Yet he noticed, as the year advanced, that Brant was growing restive. Often and more often his thoughts and words seemed to turn towards the country he had left, and at last he seemed not only ready, but eager to go.

'Art tired of our England, Joseph?' queried Colonel Guy one evening. 'Methinks that excuse you made to get away from the Duchess of Devonshire's garden party was deliberately thought up.'

'It was deliberate, Guy,' returned Brant, with his customary honesty. 'I weary of it all, and I would be prepared.'

'Prepared? For what?'

'Prepared to depart. Ah me, that it were to-morrow!' Here he sighed and moved restlessly towards the window.

'Well, it will be but three days from now, Joseph. But what is the matter? Surely no one hath affronted thee?'

The Indian smiled and shook his head. 'No, no. Everyone has been, and is, as always, exceedingly kind and hospitable. It is not because of anything here that my heart doth feel unrest. It is—over there!'

He was leaning against the casement, now staring earnestly out towards the westering sun, and Colonel Guy was frankly surprised.

'What! back in Canada? But, Joseph, old fellow, all is well there. My Catherine hath written by every packet and told the news. Even to thee personally she hath written twice, because she guessed that thou wouldst know at first hand of thy young wife's welfare, and Moon-Bow herself cannot——' here he faltered, rightly sensing what must be a source of pain to the proud Christian now, that his chosen partner was still incapable of writing, or of reading what he wrote.

But now he only nodded gravely. 'I know,' he said, 'thy Catherine is, as always a sweet and inspiring soul, and she hath said many things to hearten and assure me, and yet—and yet——'

'And yet what, Thayendanegea? Come, tell thine old friend! What is it that disturbs this gallant heart?'

Again the Englishman's kind hand rested on the broad shoulder, and the Indian's noble, rather tragic face was turned towards him with a look of more than mere affection, as he answered:

'Maybe it is what she hath not said, that doth disturb me so!'

CHAPTER VIII

In the fortified city of Montreal, Catherine Johnson and her household were doing their best under difficult and rapidly changing conditions. It was the beginning of the Empire Loyalist migration, that vast exodus of determined and dauntless people, who, while they no more agreed with the mistaken administration of the American Colonies, by a stupid and arrogant autocracy at home, than did the most rabid of the Revolutionaries, yet insisted that 'fighting was not the solution', and that they 'were law-abiding citizens, friends of the British Government, believing in, and insisting upon, the right to petition and every other legitimate and constitutional way of obtaining what they believed to be right and fair, as loyal subjects of their King'.

The suffering of these brave, high-souled people is an epic of endurance and British pluck that can never be forgotten. Though their only crimes were the adherence to principles, honest as they understood them, and an unswerving conviction, yet they were subjected to a persecution as savage and unreasoning as any which disgraced medieval days in the Old World. Recorded history has exposed grave acts of cruelty on both sides. Even at this distance in history, it is hard to determine which was more blameworthy, for, on the principle that 'two wrongs never did make one right', both had much to be ashamed of. But the Loyalists were the losers, faced with the alternative of submitting to a stronger but unrespected authority, or being evicted from their hard-won homes, and journeying, with little else than they could carry, towards the primeval vastness of scarce-discovered Canada. Few of them hesitated. They made their choice without fear or temporizing, nor were the wanderers to be found only among those of hardy background. Cultured gentlefolk were among them, delicate women, refined and unused to exposure, many with little children. Some of them found their way in small, then increasing, numbers to those parts of the Dominion called Nova Scotia and New Brunswick; thousands upon thousands, by boat, ox-cart, and quite often on foot, found their way to the great cities of Quebec and stately Montreal, intent on penetrating farther into Upper Canada.

It was among these that Catherine found her work, and never had she expected so much to be required of her. Her house, one of the larger, more pretentious houses of the city, was a social centre from the time of their arrival, and with the ever-increasing stream of new arrivals, it became even more so, as days passed on.

Catherine Johnson was a conscientious woman, who believed that a loyal wife's duty included frequent letter-writing to her absent husband; consequently every vessel that departed from that port carried several missives to Colonel Guy.

Day after day she watched the fugitives from the upper windows of her grey stone house upon the river front, hastening through the woods on the opposite side of the river, pausing not at all till they had obtained boats, barges, rafts, anything that would float, to transport them safely to the shelter of the city. Sometimes they sailed up the bosom of the river itself, out of the grey dawn mists, or up the path of the sunset, paddling their way painfully mostly, dressed in rags, faint with hunger, and often cruelly scarred. Yet they came confidently, no atmosphere of defeat brooded over them, and always in their eyes shone the same high purpose, the questioning, patient look, characteristic of the British in distress or perplexity, a look expressive of sorrow, but which nevertheless sees beyond it, and a resolution which death itself cannot shake.

Such were the people of Canada who earned the ' Marke of Honour ', the right, by decree to be ' distinguished by the letters U.E. affixed to their names, alluding to their great principle, the unity of the Empire '.

To such refugees Catherine gave ' open house '. She tended the sickly, clothed where she could, soothed the agitated, stimulated and commended those who, quick at the rebound, were anxious to go on to the land's untamed portions and hew for themselves new homes beneath the British Flag. In all this she was assisted by Kate Tourturelle. Quick at her studies, willing and patient, the Mohawk princess tried her best to aid the unfortunates of her adopted nation. And she succeeded well, for her charm and tact won their confidence, and her knowledge of ancient tribal resources also proved useful. Thus, when some Loyalist family, after brief respite in, or near, the Johnson home, prepared to move on again, either to the north or west, it was Kate who went among them, observing, advising, mentally noting missing equipment that was needed and reporting the same to her adopted mother. It was she who taught the women some ancient Indian arts, such as the dressing of deer-hide to make clothing, the art of making ornaments of berry seeds, or bone, and native ideas which might relieve the difficult sort of cooking and housewifery. Many of these women from well-furnished homes were reduced to one-roomed cabins, with roughly made furniture of logs, and open fires, and Kate, between her studies, sandwiched in this much needed work of merciful instruction.

She was progressing splendidly at the Ladies' School, so much so, that the kindly Sisters of Mercy in charge there spoke in glowing terms of her prowess to Catherine, who in her turn was frank and fond in her praise. But Kate merely smiled modestly, scarcely commenting, and seemed more absorbed in her self-appointed task than ever.

Once Catherine Johnson remonstrated with her, gently, for working too hard, but the girl answered quietly, ' There was a day, Mother mine, and not so long ago, when your white hands took me, an orphaned Indian savage into the haven of your love. And if by serving these your people, I can in any way repay, shall I not do so?'

' But, my dear,' said the lady with very real emotion, ' it was not I who found you; it was—— '

' I know,' returned Kate serenely. ' It was—he. And has he not even more cause to reverence thee and thine? Hence is my obligation doubly mine.'

Thus it was that Catherine realized how, though no word on the subject passed between them since the night of Brant's departure, the flame still burned in the Indian girl's heart, who felt herself not only under moral obligation to her own benefactor but to those who had blessed the man she loved, as well.

' Kate, my child,' demurred Catherine Johnson, fearful of such wholesale devotion. ' There are, alas, bad people among the English, or any other White people, for that matter.'

The girl nodded. ' I know,' she answered calmly, ' are

there not bad people among the Red Men, whether they be Mohawks, Senecas, or—or—others?'

Lady Catherine wondered a little at the slight falter, the more so as her companion's face seemed so grave, but just then one of her many duties called her away, and the subject was dropped.

Kate Tourturelle had much to disturb her.   Conscientiously as she had undertaken her other duties, so she had tried to cultivate the friendly confidence of Moon-Bow. For Brant's wife still remained a member of the Johnson household, and everyone made much of her, not only for the sake of her gallant husband, but because of her own amazingly beautiful face and appealing ways.   Kate, fiercely loyal, inclined indeed to condemn herself because of her own secret love, sought earnestly to gain the girl's friendship, for she had a fancy that in serving the woman he had chosen, she could best serve him. Catherine Johnson, while aware of this quixotic devotion, said little but observed much, and Kate pursued her course, fetching and carrying for the obviously frail Moon-Bow, seeking her companionship on all occasions, and indeed proving herself to be an affectionate and much-to-be-desired friend.

The handicap to all this, however, was Moon-Bow herself. For some reason she began to shun the Mohawk girl, and indeed seemed frankly uncomfortable in her presence.   Lady Catherine rightly attributed this to the strong contrast growing ever and ever apparent between them, for as Kate grew towards womanhood she developed a beauty of no ordinary kind, heightened by a marked spirituality and intelligence. Kate was always studying now, for she loved learning for learning's sake, and her adoption and practice of the Christian Faith was as sincere as it was beautiful. Moon-Bow, on the other hand, seemed content but to exist. She was gentle, soft-spoken, adapted herself prettily to customs of culture and refinement, but did so rather in the spirit of 'parrotting', than through any intelligent grasp of their value or significance. Also, another matter which caused her friends concern, despite gentle urgings on their part, and the part of others who admired the gallant Brant, Moon-Bow remained still woefully ignorant and even at that time could neither read nor write. Catherine herself would have been her teacher—so would Kate, and so would any of the gentle Sisters from the Seminary, but Moon-Bow would have none of it. Lessons apparently irked her, religious instruction or practice seemingly frightened, so more and more she withdrew to herself and then commenced wandering away, alone.

Kate, whose conscience was as tender as her heart, blamed herself for this. 'Perhaps', she thought, 'she knows my secret and is angry with me! Ah, wicked me, that I should cause her distress! Maybe it would be best if I should go to her, tell her of my fault, pray her forgiveness, and swear to her, yes, by the Holy Angels, that I would die to make her happy, because he loves her so!'

Whether this honest if mistaken plan would ever have been carried out can only be conjectured now, for it was that very night, as Kate stood cogitating by her open window, something happened that changed her mind for ever.

The Johnson home was a tall, square, five-storeyed building on the river front, whose courtyard sloped right down to the water's edge where there was a private landing place. It was not a tranquil night, for frayed clouds were scudding across the moon's face, and though the tide running down seemed placid enough, there was a sigh, like a half-suppressed moan in the noise of both wind and water, that presaged a storm.

Small boats often travelled up and down by day or night, sometimes a big windjammer, and quite often a fleet of canoes. Yet a solitary canoe, with one lone paddler, hugging the shore as though seeking concealment, and gliding with muffled strokes was unusual, and Kate stared at such a one with more than casual interest, especially when, as he glided near their dock, he shipped his paddle, driving his canoe ashore.

' A solitary Indian! ' thought Kate, staring intently, yet keeping in the shadow of the embrasure, ' and as I understand his dress, an Oneida! What can he want here, alone, at this hour, and so it doth appear to me—stealthily? Hark! What is that?'

A whisper of sound, a stealthy footstep, then a cloaked figure glided from the shadow of the house, skirted the moonlight, only to join the Indian in the shadows at the water's edge. Kate, fully alert now, watched keenly, her hawk-like eyes penetrating the gloom marking their movements. The two met, seemingly exchanged brief greetings; the one from the house seemed impatient about something, the other conciliatory.

Suddenly, with rapid action, the canoist boarded his craft and glided out into the river, and the cloaked figure turned towards the house. Less cautious now, it skirted a patch of moonlight, and as it did so, the hood fell back. Kate Tourturelle drew her breath sharply, for she was looking down into the face of Moon-Bow! For a long time after this, the Mohawk princess remained motionless by the window, her thoughts racing. Treachery! That was the only word that seemed to dance in red letters across her shocked imagination, and that word associated with the fair-faced wife of Joseph Brant! Yet what other word could describe the incident? A lone messenger by night, received stealthily under cover with reluctance that suggested fear, the brevity of the interview, the haste of Moon-Bow to have done with it, all this added to the fact that the Oneidas, Moon-Bow's own tribe, were supposedly friends of the English and loyal to the leader, and any visitor from them to his wife, openly received, would excite no comment, nor even curiosity; all this made the thing she had witnessed more alarming.

There was little sleep for Kate that night, and next day, after much reflection, she decided to keep her own counsel, nor even confide in Catherine. Gone now were Kate's conscientious qualms, and her eyes, which so gravely studied Moon-Bow, though still kind, were serious too, and very observant.

It became her habit to spend the first hours of each night by her window, for she judged that, was the incident she witnessed part of a plan, it would very likely be repeated or else Moon-Bow would herself depart for an agreed rendezvous. And did she do so, Kate resolved that she would not travel far alone!

She had not very long to wait, for it was one night, about a week later, when again the waning moon peeked fitfully through clouds of gathering storm, that the lone canoist came down the river again, and this time Moon-Bow was waiting for him, and she quickly boarded the canoe and glided away.

The tiny craft was scarcely amid-stream when Kate Tourturelle was on the tree-shadowed bank following it, gliding from trunk to trunk, using every bush, every rock, every passing cloud, to cover her progress. Years of civilization and training seemed to slip from her like a garment. She was a daughter of the Tribe again, tight-lipped, hard-eyed, her whole storming soul raging at this black evidence of betrayal, and clamouring for revenge. Yet her face remained immobile, expressionless, as the faces of her people's daughters have been since first that race began.

On, on, they went, the frail boat bobbing like a cork against the swift outgoing tide. They were going upstream towards the Narrows and edging farther and farther from the North side of the stream. The river was at one place scarcely half a mile wide, though treacherous with hidden shoals, but the canoe by this time was just a shadowy blob as it edged farther toward the opposite shore, and the Mohawk girl did not hesitate. She knew that to make her action of any avail she must shadow them, and definitely learn their purpose, so she acted swiftly.

Catching up a log, convenient in size and shape, she waded out into the river, and by using it as a screen, was soon swimming swiftly and silently in the wake of the canoe. It was difficult and very dangerous, but Kate thought nothing of her own peril. She was intent, with the dogged concentration of her race, upon those whom she considered now her quarry. When the canoe grounded, Kate was within wading distance, well by her log, and she remained still till they stepped ashore at a place where there was the glint of camp-fires through the trees, and the sound of voices. Evidently concealment was not considered necessary here, for many came to greet them, to hail Moon-Bow by name, and evidently commend her for her action. She and her companion moved away with them with free steps, and soon they were in the camp of the Oneidas, surrounded by a ring of fierce faces, and amid the brushwood, just out of sight, crouched the listener.

Almost the first words spoken, in the familiar Indian tongue, confirmed her worst fears. Moon-Bow had journeyed there deliberately, in accordance with a pre-arranged plan, developed by means the listener could only guess at, in order to betray not only her husband but her husband's friends as well. Cold with fury, the Mohawk princess listened while the soft accents of the treacherous wife proclaimed secrets, plans, conversations which revealed—or so she thought—the weaknesses of the fortified city. In this, however, she was far astray, and it soon became evident that spite and desired revenge were the only secrets revealed in this connection, and as for the military affairs she frankly knew little about them. But Joseph Brant's personal plans were another matter. He was already the coveted prize of the enemy, and as his beloved and trusted wife Moon-Bow knew all his plans. These she now revealed, with seemingly little compunction, and it was during this part of the talk that Kate overheard the plans of the Oneidas to secede from the Six Nations Confederacy, betray their Chieftain Brant into the hands of the Revolutionists, and accept reward for their dastardly achievement.

How long she remained listening to this black plot Kate Tourturelle never knew, but suddenly Moon-Bow got panicky; it might have been something the tribe's medicine man uttered, for he was gesticulating and muttering most of the time. The sky had darkened as the talk went on, and now great drops of rain came hissing through the trees,

G

and there was the rumble of distant thunder. Moon-Bow started up, protesting that she must return, and quickly, and demanding her escort and the canoe. That son of the forest, however, having conveyed her there, seemed indifferent as to how she would get back, and before long, Moon-Bow, thoroughly afraid, and perhaps conscience-stricken, hurried back to the river alone, and leaped into her boat. Even so, Kate Tourturelle was ahead of her, crouching behind her disguising log, and up to her chin in water. The tide was running down, strongly, the rain driving, and the frail boat set off under very perilous conditions, the determined swimmer following close behind, so close indeed that once she touched the gunwale.

The storm was too furious, however, and, as the river widened near the city, the rain pelted down, half-filling the canoe and threatening to submerge it. At last it did capsize, and Moon-Bow with a shriek was hurtled into the torrent, only to be caught in a desperate grip, hauled to the side of the overturned vessel, and pushed upon it.

'Cling fast!' shrieked Kate Tourturelle, her voice scarcely heard in the howling wind, 'there's an island in a hundred yards or so!'

How the next few minutes passed she could never describe, nor by what miracle they remained alive. They were swirling downstream, down a flood lashed to fury by the storm and illuminated by the weird flashes of lightning. Moon-Bow was half dead with shock and terror, the catastrophe, her miraculous rescue, the face of her companion seen fitfully in the flashes of lightning, all combined, in her own weak, disease-shadowed mind, to suggest the fury of outraged deity. She was terror-stricken, utterly helpless, and but for Kate's watchfulness would have been

carried down like the flotsam she was. But the resolute
hands clung on, and at last her feet touched bottom, and
half-wading, half-swimming, Kate struggled ashore. Once
aground, the Mohawk princess sank down, faint with
exhaustion, and Moon-Bow crouched beside her whimper-
ing like a scared animal. Then she began to cough, low
and smothered at first, and then with long, retching gasps,
and once when she drew her hands across her lips the glint
of lightning revealed a dark stain. Kate held her close,
trying to warm her against her own tired body, and
together they crouched and shivered till the storm passed,
and the grey light of a sullen summer day came stealing from
the sea.

The tide turned, and was flowing upstream more quietly,
and Kate was waiting only long enough to gather strength,
considering the possibility of swimming the remaining
distance, supporting her charge, and so getting her back to
Johnson House as quickly as she could.

'Kate, Kate,' whispered Moon-Bow at last, between
painful coughing. 'I—I—have been very wicked. Dost
know?'

'Yes—I know,' returned the other, her face turned away.

Moon-Bow cowered and shivered, then spoke again:

'Oh—h! Dost know—all?'

'I'm afraid so, Moon-Bow!'

Both spoke in the Mohawk vernacular; then after a
spasm of coughing, Moon-Bow whispered again:

'They—they are my people, Kate!'

'And he was—thine husband, Moon-Bow,' returned the
Mohawk princess tonelessly.

'Was!—Why dost say "was"?' cried the other girl
sharply, and the other countered:

' Will he be, when thou hast confessed? '

At this Moon-Bow gave a squeal of fear. ' Confessed! No, no. I will not; you cannot make me, and he cannot know; he is away; will not come back, until—until—— '

Another spasm of coughing checked her, and Kate turned on her with burning eyes :

' Until all is done, and he is prisoner, thinkest thou? A worthy thought! Know then, vile one, that if I have to give my life ten times over, that shall never be! '

Moon-Bow cowered, covering her face with her thin hands.

' Kate, Kate Tourturelle, don't—don't look at me like that! '

But the fury of the other girl's scorn would not be withheld.

' Thinkest thou I will let thy perfidy bereave my loved Lady, or do to death a warrior so grand as he? '

And to this Moon-Bow only cowered and coughed and sobbed, pleading that she meant not to harm the White Colonel, but she was unhappy, that her husband himself was a traitor; he aspired to White Man's lore, instead of following in the lore of his forefathers. He wore White Man's garments, worshipped the White Man's God. That the tribal gods were angry, the spirits of the winds and waters, that she hadn't meant to injure him, had indeed their word that his life would be spared, but he must come back to the tribe, to his own people, sever himself from his foreign friends; but that she never meant to harm him, never meant—and so on over and over again.

CHAPTER IX

A<small>ND</small> now the deep anger of the Mohawk princess melted before the pitiful ruin she looked on. From the incoherent protests of this obviously sick girl the truth was appearing. Moon-Bow feared and hated the Christian Faith to which her husband had pledged his allegiance. The gods of her people, her tribal lore with its ghost tales and clumsy magic held her in thrall. She hated the God of the White Man, regarded Him as just another tribal deity warring with her own. As for the Christian Faith, its principles, its majestic truths, its practices, meant nothing to her, and deeply engrained in her poor, warped mind was the conviction that if she could circumvent her husband in all his plans and projects, even though she betrayed him into captivity, she would be doing a right and proper thing.

Kate of the Turtles wrung her hands. ' Oh, God ! ' she whispered, tear-filled eyes upon the cowering woman beside her, ' it is not mine to judge ! Help me to do what is right, and that regardless of mine own pain ! '

So they crouched together, while the sullen light grew brighter, and a warm wet summer day was born. Then Kate stirred and shook the other.

' Rouse thyself, Moon-Bow ! There is a canoe putting off from shore. 'Tis someone fishing, methinks. I will hail him.'

' No ! No ! ' cried the other girl, her voice a hoarse shriek, ' they will find out that we have been absent—what I have done ! '

' They must know that soon,' replied Kate, sternly sad,

and then, rearing her goodly form, she cupped her hands around her mouth and sent her call across the waters. The answer came at once, and the canoist, an Indian servant of the Johnson house, recognized them. Even his stoic countenance expressed consternation as he grounded his vessel and helped aboard the Lady Catherine's adopted daughter, and the shivering, coughing, obviously broken wife of the great Chief Brant.

So they reached home again, and then there was little chance for immediate explanation, for Moon-Bow collapsed at the door, blood trickling from her nose and mouth, and when she was put to bed and medical aid summoned, the pronouncements were too grave to admit of investigation just then.

Kate Tourturelle was physically unharmed by the adventure, but she was much exhausted, and it was not until night came again, and other skilled watchers were in the sick-room, that the Lady Catherine sought her out and very quietly requested the truth.

There was nothing to be gained by concealment now, though the indignation against Moon-Bow had melted long ago into pity and distress. So the Mohawk girl told the story, beginning from that night, scarcely a week ago, when she witnessed the treacherous meeting on the quay. Catherine listened silently, almost without comment, her hands clasping the other's in a warm, consoling grip, and her eyes never leaving the beautiful dark face before her. Then, with tears dimming her expressive eyes, Kate of the Turtles began to excuse, and next to plead for her weak rival, speaking of her pitifully, as of a child, or of someone very old, and Catherine suddenly drew her into her embrace.

' Oh. Kate, my brave, sweet Kate,' she whispered, ' if

ever reward came to humble womankind, mine is before me now! Thou art all the woman I dreamed I might make of thee, and much, much more. Set thy heart at rest, dearest one, for I will do my best for her, unworthy as she is. Maybe we can avert the trouble. Messengers must be sent to waylay them, and I will make my letters so emphatic that the Colonel will heed my warning. And yet—when they do get home—when they want to know the how, and why, and wherefore, as under such circumstances all men will—then Kate. Oh! my dear, dear Kate, how are we to tell—him?'

But many weeks were to elapse before Guy Johnson set foot in Montreal again, and then a great deal of the painful story was never told, for Moon-Bow was dead.

*   *   *   *   *   *

The return of Colonel Johnson and Chief Joseph Brant to their Canadian home came about in a manner altogether unlooked for. Even the dastardly Oneida plot would have failed, and for the same reason that Catherine's letters never reached them. The returning vessel encountered a voyage as rough as the first was calm, the ship was blown greatly out of her course, and when, after weeks of delay a landing was effected, it was not in Canada at all, but at least a hundred miles from the border, in enemy territory. Fortunately, they carried ashore with them only such things as they needed, though the Indian Chief never parted with those precious documents of the Royal Assent, but secured them on his person. The country where they landed was well wooded, and Brant's first thought was to cut across it, to the comparative security of the Mohawk Valley, which, though in conquered territory, was anything but subdued. But hasty scouts reported enemy scouts to be uncomfortably near, so Brant, unwilling to risk his friend or himself, exerted all his woodman's craft, and led the party in a northerly direction towards the St. Lawrence, and then towards Montreal, gathering up such Indian reinforcements as he could on the way. They made the journey in safety for some time, though they did encounter a remnant of the Revolutionary Forces fleeing towards their own country, and it was at The Cedars, about forty miles above Montreal, trapped between Brant's party and the British, they made their last stand. Even then the humane instincts of this truly great leader were apparent, for, making himself known to the victors, he promptly took command of the Indian allies and prevented the massacre of prisoners that seemed likely to ensue in the excitement of such a success. So it came about that, as heroes, not merely belated travellers, Colonel Johnson and his friend, Captain Brant, returned to the Johnson home.

The joy of reunion was very mixed. Lady Catherine who had spent weeks of anxious waiting, rushed to her husband's arms, laughing and weeping in her excitement, then as suddenly, and to his surprise, she started back, her eyes wide with alarm.

' Guy—Chief Brant—Joseph—where did he go? '

' Go? Why, to his apartments, I suppose. I expect he will be as anxious to see his wife as I am mine. What is the matter? ' But she was pushing him towards the door, shaking his arm in her dismay.

' Ah, no, stop him, stop him ! Do not let him go there before he knows—do not ! '

' Do not what? Knows what? Why, Catherine—— '

But in a few words she panted out the truth, and Guy with an exclamation of dismay, hurried from the room.

Even then they did their best to spare the proud man; they did not tell him of her treachery.   Catherine, who later talked with him, as he sat with bowed head between these two friends who had known and loved him so long, told only of her failing health, of her efforts to please and make herself liked, and that the end came mercifully swift and painless.   That Moon-Bow was exposed to the storm she could not conceal; that was common knowledge everywhere, but she made it out to be a misadventure, a belated pleasure trip, and then she dwelt briefly, but with honest praise on the part Kate had played in the matter.   Even while she talked, Lady Catherine felt some misgiving, for all the details Kate had missed she knew now from the dying lips of Moon-Bow herself, but she felt that the story in its entirety must be told to her husband first, because treachery and double-dealing in military affairs were too serious matters, and must first be revealed to the Colonel.

So it was later still, when the bereaved man had left them, that she told Colonel Guy all the truth, and his dismay was almost as great as her own.

'I' faith, little wife,' he sighed, 'how may I, or anyone tell him this? Yet he will have to learn! Those scoundrel Oneidas! But that she—she betrayed him——! Oh, Catherine! And it was Kate, our little Kate, whom he rescued years ago—who all her innocent life hath—— By the way, where is she?' he broke off suddenly, and looking around.

'She is residing at the Seminary,' returned Catherine quietly. 'She suggested it, and I thought it best.'

'Humph! She must be almost grown up by now.'

'Yes,' his lady nodded gravely. 'She is a woman now, and a very wise and lovely woman, too!'

' I wager her little finger is worth more than Moon-Bow ! '

And the lady smiled quietly. ' There is not, and never was, any comparison.'

Colonel Johnson looked keenly at his wife. ' Cathie—! Is it possible !—Why, where were Brant's eyes? You never really liked that marriage I know, and had he waited—— '

But the lady interposed : ' Yes. But it will not exactly do to tell him that—now ! '

' But Cathie—you had time to get over this—it happened weeks ago, you say? I'm but a rough campaigner, I know —maybe inclined to be a bit hard—but treachery in any form I loathe, and methinks it were false sympathy to let Brant go long wearing the willow for one who was so unworthy, who all the time—— '

Again the lady interrupted :

' Not so fast, impetuous man, not so fast ! Though I do concur in all thou sayest, remember for him it happened but yesterday, also I fear much should he learn the truth too harshly, because in his hurt heart he has enshrined her—as a saint.'

Colonel Johnson paced restlessly up and down, then paused to stare through the window. Presently——

' I'm wondering, Cathie—if that part of the business—is wise.'

' But why? ' she questioned, anxious-eyed.

' Just this. If we do not tell him, others will.'

' But, Guy, how can they? None know here, the whole truth, save myself, and Kate. I alone was with Moon-Bow when she—when she—— '

Colonel Guy nodded gravely. ' I know—when she died. But, Cathie, you've forgotten—the Oneidas ! When he goes, as he will, to the Council, when he calls them all to follow as they promised—what then?'

That was the problem; and as the days after the return stretched into weeks, and Brant went about his duties grave and more silent, declining all ladies' company save that of Catherine Johnson, the secret so carefully kept became a burden. Kate Tourturelle he saw not at all. Soon after his return, on considering the part she had played in the rescue of Moon-Bow, he sent her a brief letter of thanks, addressing her as though she was a little child, and it was prepared so abstractedly that he even forgot to seal it, but handed the unfolded, unaddressed sheet to Lady Catherine, requesting that she give it to the girl. Needless to say, to this Kate sent no reply.

The treachery of the Oneidas was hinted to him, as time went on, by the good Colonel who, grieved for his friend but growing indignant the more he thought about it, considered that Brant's sense of loss might be modified did he know the truth; and there was some virtue in seeking consolation elsewhere. Now Guy Johnson was a soldier, and a brave one. As an adviser in military matters also he was excellent, but in affairs of the sensitive soul of man he was frankly clumsy. That is what his wife opined later, for about that time came a difference or coolness between himself and Brant, which more than once he tried to bridge. But Brant seemed deeply offended, all conciliatory overtures he rejected, and though picking no actual quarrel, and again most emphatically declaring his loyalty to the British Crown, he removed himself and his belongings from Colonel Guy's residence, and in all save military matters avoided his company. By this time spring was approaching once more, and one day it was rumoured that Captain

Joseph Brant and his party were about to leave for a meeting
with the Six Nations of the Indian Confederacy, and that he
planned to lead them out of the sorely harried Mohawk
Valley into the lands granted them by the Crown.   When
Catherine heard of this, she hurriedly sought her husband.

'Guy, my husband, there is difference between thyself
and our friend Chief Brant, is there not?' she asked.

'Alas, yes!' he sighed, and she looked at him keenly.

'Whose fault was it?'   The question was as direct as
Catherine's eye.

He stood silent for a moment, then answered quietly,
'Mine, I expect.'

'And didst apologize?   Brave people do when they are
wrong, do they not?'

He nodded, smiling somewhat at her unwavering
honesty.   'I did, frankly.   But—but it seemed of no avail.
He accepted my words, of course, in the letter and yet——'

'Maybe he requested thee to withdraw what thou didst
hint?   Am I right?'

'Yes,' he admitted reluctantly.   'And I—couldn't,
Catherine,' he concluded.

Catherine clapped her hands half-triumphantly.   'Then
I do think I know what it was,' she cried, 'It was the
Oneidas—and Kate, and Moon-Bow, and Kate, over and
over again, was it not?'

And he nodded, half-shamed, half-abashed at her perception.   'Yes,' he said, 'it was.'

Catherine stood looking at him, shaking her head re-
provingly.

'Oh, my dear, well-meaning, but big, blundering
husband!' she sighed.   'No wonder he went away in a
huff.   Were he not our own true-hearted Chief he might

have done worse, and then ye would have set a price on his head and called him " traitor "! As things are, go now, find Dr. Stewart for me; the good man hath recently taken residence in Montreal. Bring him to me at once, and also prepare to spare us Sergeant Jenks. I will need that good old fellow for some months. Go quickly and at once, for Captain Brant's cavalcade leaves very soon, and I have much to do.'

'But Catherine, what art thou about?' he demanded, but she waved him away.

'I am trying to repair thy foolish work!' she cried. 'Now, haste thee.' Then she hurried from the room.

When the much mystified Colonel returned with the good scholar, who had been Brant's schoolmaster nearly twenty years before, he found his lady completing rapid, yet very thorough preparations for somebody's journey. She greeted their guest eagerly, and drew him towards her small withdrawing-room. 'Welcome, reverend sir. Thy promptitude is gratifying, for we have much to do. Guy, dear husband, spare, I beg of thee, two good horses for Dr. Stewart, a mount, a sturdy pack-horse, also one for Sergeant Jenks, and bid him prepare. They will be needing them shortly. Come, Dr. Stewart.'

Then before her amazed husband and equally amazed guest could reply, she drew the good cleric into the withdrawing-room and shut the door. Their conference was a long one, or so thought the Colonel who, after staring in perplexity at that definitely closed door, hurried off to the selection of the horses she required, also to the instruction of Sergeant Jenks, who, very grizzled nowadays, but still remarkably fit, was soon on hand and seemingly ready for anything.

At last the door opened and the two came out, Lady Catherine with a triumphant smile and the clergyman more grave, somewhat anxious looking, but with slight amusement at the Colonel's obvious perplexity. He looked over the waiting horses, now laden and ready, nodded approvingly at the doughty sergeant, then clapped the Colonel on the shoulder.

' Thanks for thy so speedy preparations, Colonel. Though Brant's cavalcade moves out so soon, methinks I can come up with him.'

'Brant—what—you?' ejaculated the Colonel, and the other nodded.

' Yes, I think after what thy good lady hath revealed to me, it were best that I stood by my old pupil's side in what lies ahead of him. Ah, Jenks, old scout! Art ready to adventure forth with me?'

' To the ind uv the arth an' back again, if ye so desire, sorr!' returned the imperturbable Jenks. ' Though it's meself that made ready in such a whirl Oi'm not sure yit if Oi'm comin' or goin'! But the sooner we starts the better.'

' I will but return to my lodging and but briefly, and then—— '

' Thin we must drive like Jehu av old, sorr, for Captain Brant and his men went through the fortifications an hour ago!'

' So soon!' ejaculated Dr. Stewart with a start. ' Then we have not a moment to lose! Farewell, Colonel. My Lady, trust me—I will not fail. Jenks, good fellow, mount at once, we must be gone.'

It happened so quickly that the echoes of their receding hoof-beats were dying away before Colonel Johnson turned to stare inquiringly at his wife. Quietly she took his arm and led him back into her withdrawing-room. 'I told him all,' she explained, carefully closing the door. 'It is necessary in the face of Joseph's purpose, for where he hath resolved to go, cruel awakening awaits him, which I had hoped to mitigate, had I had time. But cruel lips will speak, treachery is abroad, and Guy, my husband, I have lived long enough among these people to dread the consequences of a Mohawk's wounded pride. No, he must have somebody beside him, someone to whose voice he will listen until his anger cools and he is sane again. And who better could there be than the one who guided him from the place where my poor efforts left off? As the good doctor's wise teaching guided our growing Thayendanagea through the mazes of half-understood religion, so shall his wise counsel steady him, that the black night of paganism may not again descend on his sore-wounded soul.'

CHAPTER X

WHEN Dr. Stewart and his attendant caught up with Brant's cavalcade, that gentleman was frankly surprised, but not a little pleased. It was some years since he had seen his old tutor, nor had he, since his own return, become aware that the reverend gentleman resided in Montreal. Now, to have him join the party sharing the journey and his expedition to his people was something entirely to his liking. Brant had decided that the time was come to lead his people away from a land no longer theirs to another country beneath the shelter of the British flag, and he was going to rally them for that purpose. Lady Catherine, with her womanly perception, realized that the old missionary was likely to prove a guardian angel to the gravely beset leader, and so they travelled together, the good doctor carefully concealing his apprehension, and encouraging Brant to talk about himself, his plans and all kindred subjects likely to give relief of mind and ease to a very sore heart. Sergeant Jenks shadowed them closely, and though Stewart had confided something of the matter to him, he was as immobile as one of Brant's own race, and seemingly saw, heard, and said—nothing.

Their destination was the village of Onondaga, New York, where most of the Six Nations Confederacy assembled for conference in times of stress. The Circle of Wisdom around the Great Council Fire was one of the important tribal ceremonies, for that fire had burned for many decades, and one of the biggest problems confronting this enlightened leader was how to convince the simple-minded people that another and just-as-effective fire could be kindled in their own home. Even at this his resourceful mind remained unruffled, and, upon their arrival late one night, he gave rapid orders, orders that sent some of his company scurrying into the surrounding woods with the early dawn and coming back laden with dry, resinous branches, which they cut into convenient lengths.

At last came the hour of the assembly, when the tribes drew together, headed each by the chiefs, and by the Confederacy's Chief, Little Abraham. They were all in their full regalia, and Captain Brant, by whose side Dr. Stewart remained with a marked tenacity, proceeded to address them.

He reviewed the troubles of the last few years, he dwelt sadly, but honestly, on the astonishing spirit of hate that was engendered between members of the white race. He compared it to the ill that would inevitably befall any one tribe or family who lived in perpetual enmity with another; then he emphasized the misery that was sure to descend as a result, on the innocent children of both parties. He compared at length the aggressors and defenders in this quarrel, and praised the fortitude of those who, though they had lost everything, were yet willing to go out into the Unknown, risking persecution, hardship, even death itself, for the sake of their loyalty to the British flag. He told of their journeying with little more than they could carry, often with no adequate guides, across the uncharted wilderness to the untamed lands of the North. 'Not like you shall be, were they led,' he continued, speaking of courage in the Mohawk tongue, 'with your families and possessions gathered around you, journeying in companies as numerous as the leaves, in the Moon-of-the-ripening-berries. Nor like you will, did they find welcome awaiting them, with

H

rich territory along the river bank, a territory as rich and life-giving as this you leave behind. They went in hazard, not knowing whither they went, or what might await them there. But you, you shall be prosperous. You shall not merely exist, dependent on the air, the wind, the sun, the storm for your blessing or bane. I, your brother and your champion, have knelt before the exalted chair of the Great White Chief, who dwells over the vast waters that come from the sun-rising. I have his sacred promise here——' and he held the Royal Charter aloft, ' and that which he has promised, he will of a surety perform.'

The effect of this speech seemed all that could be desired. The grave-visaged leaders of the Mohawks, the Senecas, and the Cayugas, bowed dignified heads, and gave their customary terse exclamation which the White Man has interpreted as a grunt. The Chief of the Tuscaroras lighted and pulled at the Peace Pipe, in token of his agreement, and handed it to an equally willing brother of the Onondagas; only the representative of the Oneidas remained motionless, seemingly unimpressed, and glancing slyly ever and anon at the unresponsive figure of Chief Little Abraham, leader of them all.

Joseph Brant had turned in this direction more than once, with a look of some surprise The Oneida was the brother of his late wife, Moon-Bow, and while he was accustomed to the practised unemotionalism of his people, he had expected warmer co-operation from this quarter. There was no sign, however, save that glance of meaning between the sulky one and Chief Little Abraham, and then that worthy spoke up, tersely, but with finality.

' We will not go,' he said. ' The Six Nations like not thine offer, O Thayendanegea!'

If a whip-lash had struck him across the face, Joseph Brant could not have recoiled more sharply. But he had no need to speak. The representatives of the other tribes and the onlookers to a man, burst out in cries of dissent and protest so loud as to leave no shadow of doubt. But charges and counter-charges were hurled bitterly to and fro, and during the hub-bub that followed the bitter truth was revealed to the Indian leader that his late wife's people were the sole trouble-makers, and that the only thing to do was to accept their desire to secede. Even though he reasoned with them, and finally accepted their withdrawal patiently enough, the indignation of the rest remained, and soon, by unanimous agreement, they had deposed the double-dealing Chief Little Abraham from supreme authority and had elected Joseph Brant in his stead.

At any other time such an honour would have thrilled him, but his heart was grieved now, and moreover tormented by a thousand doubts and half-forgotten memories. A certain lack of detail concerning Moon-Bow's end, the strange compassion in Lady Catherine's recent attitude towards him, Colonel Guy's clumsily put but now significant hints, added to the sudden arrival and tenacious presence of Dr. Stewart and the Sergeant, all these took on new meaning. He pushed them aside resolutely, however, and with a few brief words gave orders for instant march on the morrow.

Teepees were to be struck, families to gather possessions and personnel carefully together, and the Council Fire was to be extinguished last of all.

It was here that Chief Little Abraham spoke again, bitterly, spitefully, to the banished Oneida at his side, and that worthy spoke up, an ugly expression on his lowering face.

'The fire-gods will be angry,' he snarled, 'if you stamp out that which must be born again. For many summers and many winters has our Council Fire been blazing; it has been the light of our wisdom, and if it dies now, though ye trek into the Setting Sun, ye shall be as a people witless and without reason.'

'Is that all which deters my brother?' inquired Thayendanegea, willing to conciliate. 'Believe me, in that better land I myself will teach of a better God, who will not be angry for such childish things. As for the Council Fire, it shall not die, and ye shall take it with you. Behold these branches I have caused to be cut and laid in readiness. From the Council Fire shall be kindled Six Torches, and there are many more times six to catch up the flame when these are burnt. So shall the flame be kept alight and carried before us, on, on, on, through all our long, Northern trek, across the dividing waters and so into the land that hath been promised to us and our children for ever.'

'Just as the Pillar o' Fire led the Children o' Israel of Ould—ye copper-hided haythen,' muttered the imaginative Jenks suddenly and *sotto voce*, for he did not like the gathering wrath on the Oneida's face.

Dr. Stewart heard him, however, and whispered in English: 'I fear there is going to be trouble, Jenks—the secret's coming out!'

'Hiven forbid, sorr! For the Captain will go wild!'

But the rebel was out for mischief; maybe he guessed that Brant was in ignorance of the whole truth, and the missionary whispered again and hurriedly: 'If necessary, punch him in the mouth, Jenks—that Oneida, I mean. I'll look after Brant.'

'I will, sorr—do the saints preserve—Oh, Achem! Here it comes!'

The Oneida drew himself to his full height, strode forward, and confronted the astonished Brant. 'Scheming, smooth-tongued, double-mouthed as ever, Thayendanegea,' he cried. 'Thou who crawlest in the White Man's shadow, and would fain have thy people fawn as thou hast fawned. Thou struttest in their war gear, like to the stripling who dons his father's weapons and cries, "Behold me, I am grown." Small wonder is it to all who know, that Moon-Bow wept at thy perfidy, thy vile ambitions, and for fear of thee and thy foreign plots fled back to us— her people and her friends!'

'Speak not of Moon-Bow; she is dead!' commanded Brant hoarsely, his numbed mind scarcely taking in the purport of the words.

'Dead, is she?' retorted the other. 'And why? Strange that she should die so suddenly after she had thrown thee and thy falseness to the winds, and chosen to reveal to us——'

A snarl like that of a maddened animal cut the speaker short. Thayendanegea, his face scarcely human, leaped forward, tomahawk in hand. But Sergeant Jenks was before him. His hammer-like fist shot out and the Oneida went down before it like a log, and on the same instant Dr. Stewart seized the infuriated man and held him back.

'Forbear!' he cried, though speaking in the Indian tongue. 'Remember, thou art a soldier of the King!'

But it was a wild man that he held! Gone were the years of culture, the trappings of civilization that had extended over years. It was a son of the wilderness, hard-eyed, cruel-lipped, who struggled with him, seeking to throw off the detaining hands, and who had only enough perception left to realize the grip was friendly, and to refrain from doing the man harm.

'Let me go!' he commanded thickly, also using the Mohawk speech. 'Thou runnest much risk, White Man! There is stain upon mine honour, and——'

But Stewart, exerting his remaining strength, forced the other around until he could stare deep into the flaming eyes. Then he clutched at both the sweating shoulders, and spoke again, sonorously, in English: '" Thou shalt not kill "!' he said. '" Thou shalt not kill "!'

There was an awful pause; the onlookers remained as though carved in stone, while the Council Fire flickered on the strangest scene it had ever beheld. It was a White Man, elderly, past his greatest strength, who was exorcising the devil of madness that raged in their Forest Champion.

And he prevailed! The proud head drooped, the flaming eyes softened, became sane again, steady, but inexpressibly sad. The tense muscles relaxed, but the crowding doubts became a certainty, so that he was scarcely surprised, as in answer to his low-breathed question: 'Tell me, is what he stated, true?' the answer came reluctant, but steadily, 'Yes.'

Thayendanegea turned towards his followers, his proud, dignified self once more, though one hand rested rather heavily on the missionary's shoulder. Briefly he repeated his orders that the exodus commence on the morrow, glanced at the prostrate Oneida whom Jenks had kept so by the simple process of planting one heavy foot on his chest, and ordered him and his tribe out of the camp immediately. Then he turned towards his own tent, pitched at a specially chosen spot, and drew his companion with him.

Once concealed beneath its friendly folds, he sank down heavily, his face buried in his hands. 'Tell me all about it,' he said in muffled tones. 'Methinks I have been spared by well-meaning friends. Old friend and teacher, tell me all.'

So the gentle missionary told the whole story as he had heard it from the Lady Catherine, dwelling as lightly as he could, yet honestly on Moon-Bow's treachery, and quietly, though with an admiration he could not conceal, on the gallantry of Kate. Thayendanegea heard him to the end, without comment, and then he raised his head.

'I have wronged my friends,' he sighed. 'Good-natured Guy Johnson especially, but I will write to him, when this business is over, and ask his pardon as a true man should. But for the lady—the lady in whose hands mine honour was so safe, though I, proud fool that I was, saw nought of it, I can but hope that she in her so great wisdom will understand, when I say I cannot yet know what is in my heart to speak, for I cannot trust myself to speak.'

'Wilt rest thee now, Joseph?' asked the missionary after a long silence. 'Methinks it were wise for one with such responsibility to get some sleep.'

The Chieftain shook his head. 'I cannot rest yet, my brain feels on fire. Remember, I have only just realized that she—But thou art a-wearied——' he broke off. 'Rest thee, though, I do pray thee, by my side.'

'No, no, I will watch with thee, Joseph, that is if thou wilt have me.'

The other smiled rather sadly. 'I do welcome thy companionship, for my heart is heavy now, and inside my soul there war two angels, one white as light, the other blacker than the pit.'

'My poor Joseph, how may I best help thee?' cried the old teacher tenderly.

'That I will tell to thee,' answered the Red Man gravely, 'when thou hast helped me first to raise this treasure.' He was kneeling on the floor as he spoke, beside the old tree stump around which he had insisted that his tent be pitched. Now he commenced digging into the ground with his hunting knife, and so at last he lifted a large flat stone, and from the cavity beneath it, drew a black, nail-studded box. From his neck he produced a small key attached to a chain, fitted it into the lock, and lifted the lid. Then he drew out several objects wrapped in woollen cloth. 'The Silver Vessels for the Holy Communion,' he explained, in answer to Dr. Stewart's surprised inquiry. 'These were given to my revered father the Great Chief Tehowaghwengaraghkin, by the Queen Anne. That is a long time ago now, but with her own royal hands did she bestow them, to be used and venerated by my people for evermore. They must go with us, our most sacred treasures now, to glow maybe once more upon a Christian altar, insignia of better days.'

He was unfolding the wrappings as he spoke, and now he placed them reverently, platters and chalices complete, on a low bench nearby. Then as sudden he sank down again into a crouching position, his proud head bowed on the older man's knee. 'Tell me,' he pleaded in muffled accents, his strained face buried in his twitching hands, 'tell me, ere the devils tear at me again, of that One who made these sacred—who could forgive the greatest wrongs. Tell me again of the Lord Christ I try to serve, that even though now I writhe in inward torment, I may remember Him, and so may keep my soul.'

CHAPTER XI

THE exodus of the Five Nations Confederacy of the Indian Tribes, from the Mohawk Valley, New York, to the territory promised them in Canada, is now a matter of history. Many incidents have been related concerning it, some true, others exaggerated. Doubtless there were times when the brave Thayendanegea almost despaired in the stupendous task to which he was dedicated. Not only were the people he championed uncertain, or at best apathetic, but some of his British friends, though on the whole well-meaning, were slow to respond, and often crowded his urgent pleas under the ponderous machinery of official red-tape. Yet all commended his nobility, his resolution, and personal exertions in the cause he believed in, as well as his attachment to the British Government, and it was not a little owing to Brant's personal popularity that the tract of land on the banks of the Grand River from Lake Erie to its source was granted to them. For one hundred miles it ran, fertile rolling country extending from six to ten miles on either side of the river, and this, according to the Treaty, they were to 'possess and enjoy for ever', even though certain legal 'strings' to the grant carried with them disappointment, and, from the holders' point of view, handicap. Still, Brant laboured patiently, and though he did not number the art of public speaking among his accomplishments, yet he pleaded on occasions so fearlessly and well, as to achieve most of what he sought. His entire undertakings were the labour of years, however, and his first duties on their arrival were to encamp his people on various parts of the Reserve, and inspire them towards the development of communal and family life.

His own holding, granted him by Crown Patent, as a mark of kingly favour, was a 3,400-acre tract of land at Wellington Square, near the Head-of-the-Lakes. Here he planned to build a noble house, for he ever remembered, and with admiration, the stately homes in England, and had grown to love them well. That, however, would have to wait, for his own loved people needed all his attention. It was well that the foresight of Lady Catherine had placed Dr. Stewart at his side, for that good old cleric aided and advised with a cheerful patience that meant much to this warrior Chief, whose position, added to his own recent personal sorrows, placed him singularly alone. In the many conferences they held together, seated in that little army tent, after night had fallen, Brant would again express the dreams and plans he had formed in early manhood, and again, with the doctor's willing help, he would essay the translation of those portions of the Gospel he loved best, till the old enthusiasm was awake once more, and weariness and personal disillusionment were forgotten.

' We must build a church, good Doctor,' he declared one night. ' West of Montreal there is no place where White Man or Red, of the Christian Faith, may kneel in prayer. That is not good, for as we both know, no weed springs more quickly nor bears more poisonous fruit than superstition and godlessness. Not only for my people will we build this church—although it shall be called by their name, but the White Man, following in the Red Man's trail, seeking as we do, a new home, and the right to live, shall, if he so desire, worship there with us. Dost not agree with me, old friend, that now is the time to build?'

'Not a moment too soon,' agreed the doctor whole-heartedly. 'But do not stop at that, Joseph. With a church should rise a school, so that the little ones who are, or soon will be, born here, may learn intelligently what it is all about, and not regard this worship as but another form of White Man's Magic.'

'A school? H'm, yes. The Loyalist cabins are going up, verging on the borders of our domain, dotting the country from here to the mountain at Head-of-the-Lakes. Yet a school requires a teacher. And who in all our village of Ohswekan could do that? I have neither the gift, nor the leisure, and as for thee, old friend, methinks I tax thee sorely as it is. So much as I would like a school, how may we have one with none to teach?'

'Wilt leave this matter in my hands, Joseph,' responded the good cleric, kindly. 'Methinks between myself and our fair Lady Catherine, something may be accomplished.'

'Lady Catherine? God bless her!' ejaculated Brant with very real emotion; then he got up and strode to the tent door, and stood staring out into the soft darkness. When he spoke again it was in somewhat muffled tones. 'Methinks, good Doctor, that the holy angels we hope some day to behold, must much resemble her.'

So it came about that a company of late summer voyagers travelling by portage and water highways from the Head-of-the-Lakes past the Bay of Quinte, through the islands beyond, shooting the rapids of Lachine, and paddling manfully through long days and nights, arrived at the quays of Montreal, paused briefly at the Johnson House, and there delivered a packet of letters, one of which in particular seemed to afford the Lady Catherine much cogitation.

When she raised her eyes she saw her husband regarding

her with a grave, inquiring look, and she rose to greet him with a smile.

'I must visit the Seminary to-morrow, Guy,' she said, 'and talk with our little Kate.'

'Then tell her 'tis time she came home to Johnson House,' he replied heartily. 'I' faith methinks since she became a teacher there, she hath forgotten that she hath a home.'

'Nay, our Kate forgets nothing,' returned the lady. 'What she has been doing was with my knowledge and consent.'

'What bee hast in thy bonnet now, Cathie?'

'A honey bee,' she retorted archly, 'and though it may sting, yet it can carry wondrous sweetness. I may be requiring two good horses from thy stables, Guy, and, prithee, when does the next caravan start out for Upper Canada?'

'Two more horses! And 'twas but at the beginning of last year I parted with three of my best! Who is it thou wouldst be sending into Upper Canada now?'

'A schoolmistress,' returned the lady gently, and glided out, leaving him speechless.

It was next day that Lady Catherine Johnson's coach and pair stopped outside the Seminary for Young Ladies, where Kate of the Turtles had been employed for over a year, and greeting the shy, somewhat flustered woman who admitted her, in her own, kind manner, Catherine requested to be conducted into the presence of Mademoiselle Catherine Tourturelle.

The young woman who rose to greet her might have been a daughter of some noble French House, so elegant, so poised, so sure of herself was she. By this time about twenty-one, tall, exquisitely formed, the Mohawk princess would have put many of her paler sisters to shame, so noble was the proudly poised head, so faultless the rich complexion, so abundant the gleaming hair of jet black, which she wore piled high after the latest Parisian mode, and with drop curls on her shoulders. Yet her eyes remained her most compelling feature: dark, deep wells of light, they were intelligent, searching, and above all, quick and kind. Her every movement was graceful, and when she spoke, her voice was a musical contralto.

'Mother, beloved!' she said, coming forward, long, artistic hands outstretched. 'How wondrous a surprise!'

The Lady Catherine kissed her with very real affection, then holding her at arms' length looked at her keenly.

'How beautiful thou art, my Kate!' she cried. 'I' faith, my poetic-minded husband were like to nickname thee "Golden-Rose"!'

Kate laughed a little and blushed, as the lady continued: 'Thou art like to set many a gallant heart aflame, my Kate. Art sure thou hast not so done?'

The blush deepened, but Kate shook her head.

'I know not, Mother beloved, if I have done so—and I care not,' she answered.

The lady was still regarding her keenly.

'Thou art an unbelievably rare soul, Kate. Is it possible that one love, and one only, still dominates thy life?'

'Thou knowest it,' answered the girl in low tones. Then she looked up. 'But I cannot think that my Mother beloved came here but to ask me that,' she said.

Lady Catherine smiled. 'We understand one another, I see,' she said. 'No, my dear, I came not for that, any more than I urged thy mastery of the teacher's art as an aimless accomplishment. Thou hast done nobly, as I know from reports, and now I have come to tell thee that thy faithful days of preparation are over, and it is time.'

'Time?' repeated Kate, questioning gaze upon her.

'Yes. Time to take thy place by Joseph Brant's side, and, though he knows it not, help him to accomplish his heart's desire.'

'Thou dost mean——?'

'I mean that Dr. Stewart has written to me from the New Country of the Mohawks requesting that I seek and send a school teacher to help them in their work. Now, thou art qualified above all others that I can think of. So—wilt thou go, my Kate?'

'He—he may recognize me,' hesitated Kate, but her eyes were glowing with an eager light, and the lady answered, 'That is not very likely. It is years since he saw thee. But even if he did—he needs thy help, so, wilt thou undertake the task, Kate?'

And the Mohawk princess answered steadily, 'Yes. I will go.'

*   *   *   *   *   *

When Catherine Tourturelle, after weeks of rough travel, arrived at the Canadian Country of the Indian Confederacy, she found surprising progress had already been made. Although hardly a year had elapsed since they first took possession of their lands, some semblance of orderly living had been established. The untiring efforts of Chief Brant, Dr. Stewart, and one or two other leaders among the tribes, whose adaptability qualified them, had produced creditable results. Some of the land was broken, divided into holdings, and here and there tiny cabins were replacing the wigwams of an earlier day, promising by their very presence, an attempt at better living.

Such forward-reaching people seemed by general consent

to have gathered into their own communities, and, in other parts of the Reserve, families who clung to the older traditions congregated. They all admired Chief Brant and trusted him, and most of them tolerated Dr. Stewart, though it was only the most progressive among them who were really at ease with him. The others, though as brave in battle as their fellows, and for the most part as trustworthy, hung back, for their world seemed to be moving too fast for them, and their unwitting efforts to slow things up savoured pathetically of self-defence.

It was among both classes that the new schoolmistress found her work. Introduced as Mademoiselle Tourturelle of Montreal, the elegant, graceful, well-taught lady quite easily passed for a native of Old France, nor did even the Indians themselves seem to suspect her origin. Brant was totally unaware of it, and referred to her, as did most of her new friends, as ' The French-Canadian Demoiselle from the great city '.

It was when the next winter was departing, when breaking ice was opening waterways, the cold was less severe, and the breath of spring was sifting through the forest lands that an influx of new-comers attracted Kate, won her sympathy and ardent co-operation. They were the ever-increasing companies of the United Empire Loyalists, who, penetrating farther and farther towards the north and west, were seeking literally to hew homes for themselves from the depths of the primeval forests. They scrupulously avoided any encroachment on the Indian lands, but established themselves on those surrounding it, journeying there mostly on foot, by ox-wagon, or horse-back, often with no more than the clothes they stood up in, and equipped with the simplest tools. Kate saw among them delicate ladies with little children, standing, with eyes bleak but steadfast, surveying the unbroken lands around them, where even roofs to shelter them had to be hewn from the living trees. She mingled among them in her capacity as official from the adjoining community, and thus she saw and heard unutterable things. Women whose eyes smiled bravely at their men, though themselves drooping with sickness and fatigue, and who only gave vent to the grief they felt when their men were out of hearing. The men themselves, scarred and cripped with the war, some with cruel marks upon them that made Kate wonder about the White Man's vaunted superiority of civilization. But she welcomed all she could, cheered and encouraged them, bringing her knowledge of Indian home-building, advising here, helping there, all this in addition to the official duties that brought her there in the first place.

Of Chief Brant she saw but little, and, as Lady Catherine Johnson had suspected, he was too absorbed in his self-imposed task to recognize in her the half-grown Indian maid he had carelessly looked at years before. So Kate continued her work, establishing order and discipline in the wild little lives entrusted to her, and encouraging by diplomatic visits the co-operation of the half-doubtful mothers, making friends among the surrounding Loyalist families so that she might in turn not only benefit by their culture and experience, but promote a friendliness between the two communities which should tend to develop a closer harmony. Nor was her work without effect, for during those first long months of hardship when sometimes Government supplies were behind schedule, it was the Indians who went to the aid of their white neighbours, and in charitable good nature supplied them with food and clothes. While her life was a very busy one, yet Kate made time to write to Lady Catherine long accounts which from time to time, she managed to dispatch by caravan or canoe to Montreal.

'. . . we are but making haste slowly,' she wrote in one letter . . . ' for the main handicap we have to overcome among my people is superstition and fear. They still cannot understand why White Man's magic is not sufficient to overcome all this, and why they, who chose as they believe, the right, should have to suffer. The ideals of the Manitou, as contrasted with the God of the Christians, call forth mixed response, especially as so many so-called Christians are anything but good. They lie, they are cruel to defenceless things, and the Red Man's god teaches that it is wrong to do both. Also the plight of the Loyalists, beaten, robbed, often mutilated, fills them with amaze. That White Men should do thus to White Men passes their comprehension and but for the reaction of these new refugees our task might be harder than it is. But they are grand, these people, and I for one am proud to be as their adopted sister, and proffer them my aid. Though they have to break every foot of ground they take, must live in tiny cabins with ill-fitting doors, and windows stopped with oiled paper in lieu of glass, they never complain. They bring so little with them. Sometimes a fortunate family possesses an axe or hand-saw, sometimes a group will possess a set of tools or a cross-cut. But they are pitiably short of weapons. One group of ten families had only two fire-locks among them, but I hear a supply of these is expected soon. Also among this same group, in which were thirty-nine children, there was only one pair of shoes ! It's a stylish cabin that possesses two rooms. I have seen delicate-fingered ladies with their children, packing slabs of

I

mud and moss between the timbers of their cabins to keep the weather out, and though their cheeks are wet with tears when none are by, should any other of their company draw nigh, they brush them away in haste and begin animated talk of all they mean to do with the cherished possessions they have with them. Anybody who possesses a quilting frame or a spinning wheel is well off, but already I have suggested the usefulness of petticoats made of deerskin, and many there are who have thankfully accepted my advice.

'Near the border of our Reserve is one family who brought with them two live sheep. They are looked on as prosperous farmers and hope to succeed in raising a flock of them, and then the community will have wool. I am attending a wedding to-morrow, for our revered Dr. Stewart is to unite the daughter and son of two splendid Loyalist families, and of course the community wishes to give them a good start. The bride has quite a dowry! Six silver teaspoons which she managed to smuggle across the border in the bosom of her dress, and a cow! This was given by the bridegroom's family who succeeded in bringing two with them, and one later had a calf. She is considered quite a rich man's daughter and is to be arrayed in a bridal gown of calico. Of course I shall go to the wedding, which is to take place in the open air, for the Church of the Mohawks is, at present, only our Chieftain's dream.

'How right thou art, Mother beloved, now as always, for indeed and indeed he does not recognize me! When he met me first, he bowed low—like the prince he is— addressed me courteously, but looked on me with a stranger's eyes! For one thing, his heart is wrapped in his work, and I—though it may surprise thee not at all when I

say so—I glory in it, too. Strange, is it not, that the Thing
Beloved and the Beloved's Ideals become as one in the
heart of the Lover? Or dost thou think it strange? Somehow I see thy wise, kind eyes smiling as they scan these
words, and I see thy dear head give that little knowing shake
that I do remember and understand so well. Thou wert in
all things right, Mother beloved, true love—the only love
that shall endure—thinks not of itself, or even the satisfaction
it might gain in the glory of possession—though that might
be of Heaven itself. But it minds most the welfare of
that which it idealizes. So I am happy, I am working with
and for him. Let him continue to look on me, if he will,
with stranger's eyes, providing he is happy in his sense of
achievement, watching his life-dream materialize, while I
with my obscure though perhaps timely aid may contribute
to his happiness and so gain my reward.'

Kate had written this letter at intervals during a busy
week, and now, hastily concluding and sealing the missive
at her desk by the open window, she sat for a few moments,
chin resting on her clasped hands, and eyes a-dream. Then
she started, for a shadow fell across her desk. She looked
up, then rose hurriedly, for Joseph Brant stood before her.

But he had not recognized her—she soon saw that.
Instead, on his forehead was a puzzled frown, and he
glanced from her to the bunch of papers he held, his fine
eyebrows slightly knit.

'Pardon my intrusion, Mademoiselle Tourturelle,' he
said, bowing slightly, and speaking in his usual precise English. 'I know it is ungallant to trouble one so hard-worked,
at the end of so long a day, but I am in sore perplexity, and
much wonder if thy wise head could help me out.'

'Willing am I to try, Captain Brant. Wilt thou be

seated?' she asked, indicating by slight gesture a rough bench beside her.   And to hear her calm accents, none would guess the tumult within.

He was smoothing the bundle of papers, and now produced a badly battered pen.

'It is this translation,' he explained. 'Thou knowest maybe that I have set my heart on teaching my people the Scriptures in their own tongue?'

'I have heard so, yes,' she answered. 'It is a noble work, indeed; pray tell me how I may be of help.'

For a second he paused and glanced up, the mellow voice was so arresting, then he continued, eyes upon his notes. 'It is how to convince them that troubles me. I have translated painfully, accurately—but the result is lifeless. It seems like making them repeat so many incantations. I cannot make them feel!'

'What particular portion is it that does so perplex thee?' she asked, and he held the papers towards her.

'This, it is the Gospel of St. Luke. I am trying to tell them the Story of Christmas—as I understand it, and as it is commemorated to-day in Christian England, but somehow —somehow——'

'Maybe I can be of help,' said Kate quickly, and she rose and unlocked a small cupboard nearby. 'I caused this to be made to contain my books and papers,' she explained in answer to his look of interest. 'Here are the words of a song I plan to teach the children. It was written nigh two hundred years ago by Jean de Breboeuf, but I do think it answers thy question.'

She handed a paper to him, and to his astonishment Joseph Brant found himself reading a poem in the French tongue, which, literally translated, ran thus:

' 'Twas in the moon of Wintertime, when all the birds had fled,
That Mighty Gitchi Manitou sent angel-choirs instead.
Before their light the stars grew dim
And wandering hunters heard the hymn—
Jesus your King is born! In Excelsis Gloria.

Within a Lodge of broken bark the tender Babe was found,
A ragged robe of rabbit-skin enwrapped His beauty round
But as the hunter braves drew nigh
The angel song rang loud and high.

The earliest moon of Wintertime is not so round and fair
As was the ring of glory on the helpless Infant there,
The Chiefs from far before Him knelt
With gifts of fox and beaver pelt.

O children of the forest free,—O sons of Manitou,
The Holy Child of Heaven and Earth is born today for you;
Come kneel before the radiant Boy,
Who brings you beauty, peace and joy.'*

He was looking at her now with a light in his eyes as if
he saw some saint, and Kate, to steady the fluttering of her
heart, spoke again in tones that trembled slightly : ' If you
desire our—the people to understand, teach them the story
in the language in which they THINK, in familiar settings of
moons and forests and teepees, and a hunting-lodge. Their
minds are simple yet; they must be guided as with a White
child's picture toy. Thus, though they cannot visualize
" swaddling clothes " they quite well can understand a
" ragged robe of rabbit-skin ".'

He was on his feet now, and in his enthusiasm he caught
both her hands. ' Mademoiselle Tourturelle—I—how can
I th—— ' then he paused again, eyes widening, and examined
her face with a searching, questioning look.

* This poem was written in French in the seventeenth century and
this translation is by J. E. Middleton.

' Whence learned you all this,' he asked at length and more quietly, and Kate managed to reply, with reasonable composure, ' In Montreal.'

He was still staring at her steadily, unaware that his strong hands clasped her own; then he spoke again, almost beneath his breath. ' Kate! Little Kate of the Turtles! Can it be possible——? '

But her answer to him was like a cry of gladness. ' O Thayendanegea! Dost thou recognize me—at last? '

CHAPTER XII

THE erection of the first Protestant Church in Upper Canada was directly due to the efforts of Chief Thayendanegea of the Mohawks, that gallant gentleman known to his British friends as Captain Joseph Brant. In the district named Ohswekan was it builded, not far from where stands the modern Mohawk Institute. Just a simple little church, about sixty feet long by thirty feet wide, with a small pointed steeple, and an entrance flanked with stone coping and rough-hewn steps. Of hardwood was it builded, upon a firm oaken foundation whose beams and joists measured fourteen inches square. The floor was of maple planking, and the entire interior lined with a fragrant cedar, wrought into ornamental designs. The small font of oak and marble stood to the left of the altar, upon which at last rested the rare vessels of the Queen Anne Communion Set, and on the pulpit desk nearby was the priceless Bible. Above the altar were the Commandments inscribed in fair lettering in the Mohawk tongue, so that all who would might understand :

' Toghfaok Aghferryeh ! '—' Thou shalt not kill ! '

' Toghfaok Thaonfaghfadogea ! '—' Thou shalt not commit adultery ! '

' Toghfaok Aghfenoufkoh ! '—' Thou shalt not steal ! '

And on either side of this were inscribed the Belief in the One God, and that noblest of all prayers to Him—' Our Father '.

The appearance of the bell, housed not in the usual tall tower but in a separate structure, was a great surprise.

It was not until the church was nearly finished that Chief Brant produced it, and then confessed to the gratified missionary, that he had purchased it while in England, and conveyed it, at much cost and trouble, to this new country, hoping for such a time as was now at hand. For many years was it destined to hang there, melodious evidence of one strong man's struggle towards his ideal. It is inscribed with the name of the founder and the date. At last the silver Communion Set and the copy of the Bible were in suitable surroundings, and though all these preparations took many months, the time of the grand festival of the opening ceremony drew near, and thanks to the tireless efforts of Dr. Stewart, the Chief himself, and their faithful school-mistress, even the apathetic Indians were becoming mildly enthusiastic, and their Loyalist neighbours ardently so.

Since the day he had recognized her, the friendly co-operation of Joseph Brant was an inspiration to Kate Tour-turelle. She had worked before, but now she redoubled her efforts, among both her own people and her Loyalist friends, until her influence, far-reaching and subtle as only a woman's can be, began to produce results that astonished even him.

'I' faith, Doctor,' he remarked one day, as he and the old missionary were reviewing events together, 'it seems to me that our fair schoolmistress knows not how to become fatigued. I deemed myself fairly thorough, but she thinks of and does things I would never remember, or, if I did, think unimportant. Yet her judgement is excellent, it far outstrips my own! Our Indian women are hardy, I know, yet many would sag beneath such a strain, but Kate—Mademoiselle Tourturelle, I mean—seemeth to thrive upon it.'

'Who can find a virtuous woman—her price is above rubies——' quoted the old teacher, regarding his friend with a somewhat quizzical smile, and Joseph Brant fell silent, and rather suddenly turned away.

But he was watching her at a distance; he noted her influence among her sister women, her wise kindness to the Loyalists, whose lot would have been harder but for her. She it was who guided them to where the wild raspberries grew, and taught them how to preserve the wild plums and pungent crab-apple. She initiated them into such wood-craft as would lessen their danger of becoming lost, and how to search for and choose the resinous pine branches suitable for torches or fuel.

She was still hard at work when the time of the church opening arrived. It was in the fair Canadian summer-time, but because for some time now new trails were being blazed, and then established, from the cities of the East, it had been possible for Colonel Johnson and his lady to journey to the Head-of-the-Lakes, and so up country to be present at the ceremony. Brant and the Colonel had not met since that time, nearly three years ago, when they parted in coldness, in Montreal. But all was forgotten now, for letters had passed between them, and the difference was ended, so that when they clasped hands on the landing place of Macassa Water, it was as old friends.

Over the Lady Catherine's hand, her one-time protégé bent with very deep affection, and in a low, almost broken voice, tried to thank her for her part in it all, but she checked him gently, commending him in her old sweet, under-standing way, and making him sure she meant it, that his success was all the reward she craved, and that from her beloved Indian prince and princess she desired nothing more than that they would go on, from strength to strength. Then she moved forward to greet Kate Tourturelle, who, with their missionary friend, was also there, and they repaired together to Wellington Square where the Chief's own house, overlooking fair Macassa Bay, was nearly finished.

It was after the first joys of reunion were modifying into placid content that Joseph found himself in the company of his two friends, glancing often and more often to a spot just a few yards away, where two lovely women were conversing together—Kate, with her rich colouring, her lofty brow, and soft, though brilliant eyes, and stately Lady Catherine, whom maturity had but enhanced, and whose still bright hair, like a golden aureole, framed a face wise and womanly and beautiful as an angel's.

Their conversation was inaudible, though plainly it was profound, for the kind eyes of the elder lady were fixed on the other with a half-quizzical smile, and suddenly the proud head of the Indian princess drooped a little, the long lashes shadowed the warm cheeks, upon which a rosy glow deepened. Her lips were smiling, however, though she shook her head. Then the elder lady spoke again and the long lashes lifted in a sudden, swift, yet womanly-wise glance, maybe such a glance as Ruth of the Moabites gave when her mother-in-law Naomi uttered those cryptic words, ' Sit still, my daughter—for the man will not be in rest until—— '

*   *   *   *   *   *

And now came the date of the opening ceremony when Indian people from far and near thronged into the church, and Loyalist neighbours came to swell the ranks. For the first time the sweet summons of the bell called them to worship and they came promptly, some with intelligence and enthusiasm, others with curiosity, none with fear. The Indian children filed in, too, under the watchful eyes of older girls, for Kate Tourturelle this day did not conduct them. Hers was another duty, embodied in another surprise, for Lady Catherine, recalling Brant's long-ago commendation of organ music, had brought, though with much labour and expense, a small reed organ, which she presented to the church. And Kate of the Turtles was seated at this, her long golden fingers charming music from its ivory keys. Chief Brant knew nothing of this latest gift till he entered the church, but when he heard and saw, his proud face quivered, and he gripped the hands of his friends and pressed them hard.

Then the ceremony began. The children opened it, singing a hymn which Kate had taught them, one which she knew Brant loved, because he had heard it once before under circumstances he could never forget.

' God is the Refuge of His Saints.'

The first prayer ever uttered in the first Protestant church of Upper Canada was brief, but so full of inexpressible emotion, as to make it very beautiful. Every head was bowed, some easily, as to custom, others awkwardly and in awe, but all in reverence, and then the quiet, tender voice of Dr. Stewart arose, speaking in English, while sentence by sentence the deep accents of Chief Brant translated his words—' O Divine All Father, from the ends of the earth we have come, some from rich homes wherein we thought we were secure, some from rich lands where in peace and plenty we lived and hoped to live as our fathers did before us. But all these have passed from us, there have been hard days, times of pain and loss, and many tears. Now we are living together side by side, both Red Men and White, trying to find peace and plenty again, and knowing we can only do so if we seek it from Thy Hands——'

On, on, went the tender voice and the faithful tones of the translator. Then there was a pause and from the roughly fashioned desk the preacher lifted the Book, upon the pages of which lay a closely written manuscript. It was Joseph Brant's translation of one of the most beautiful of all prayers—'Almighty Father to Whom all hearts are open . . .'

And at last the ceremony was ended. To the slow, sweet strains of the organ the people filed out, but Kate continued playing long after the church was empty, for her heart was very happy that day. So much had been accomplished. The weary years of preparation, disappointment, and doubt seemingly slipped away, almost from remembrance, or to be thought of in perspective as the necessary scaffolding for the structure that was to be. There was so much to be done, a lifetime of earnest endeavour, with endless possibilities among friends old and new.

She did not hear the light step in the aisle, nor realize she was not alone, until a shadow crossed the long, warm hands that caressed the keys. Then she looked up, and she saw him standing there—standing with the light behind him, and on his face the look she longed for most.

' Catherine ! '—He had never called her that before, but somehow it seemed all gloriously right, and she looked up at him, a smile upon her lips, still playing softly.

' Yes, Thayendanegea,' she answered.

Both spoke in the Mohawk tongue, and now his strong hands closed over hers, lifted them from the keyboard, and drew her up to him.

'I had to come back,' he said, 'because there is something else—something I must tell to thee—alone.'

The jewel-like eyes never left his face, the parted lips still smiled, as she answered softly: 'I am listening—my Prince.'

'Catherine, I have been very slow at understanding—but now I do know. Wilt thou come to me, my dear, and share my life as thou hast shared my work? Wilt thou wed with me, sweet Catherine?'

And she answered, very tenderly, 'Yea, I will; for, oh, my Thayendanegea! I do know that I have loved thee all my life.'